SIX STEPS TO A GIRL

SIX STEPS TO A GIRL

Sophie McKenzie

Simon & Schuster

This edition published 2014

First published in Great Britain in 2007 by Simon and Schuster UK Ltd,
A CBS COMPANY

1 3 5 7 9 10 8 6 4 2

Simon & Schuster UK Ltd
1st Floor, 222 Gray's Inn Road
London WC1X 8HB

Simon & Schuster Australia, Sydney
Simon & Schuster India, New Delhi

A CIP catalogue record for this book
is available from the British Library.

PB ISBN: 978-1-47112-150-0
EBook ISBN: 978-0-85707-667-0

This book is a work of fiction. Names, characters,
places and incidents are either the product of the author's imagination
or are used fictitiously. Any resemblance to actual people living
or dead, events or locales is entirely coincidental.

Typeset in Times by M Rules
Printed and bound by CPI Group (UK) Ltd, Croydon, CR0 4YY

www.simonandschuster.co.uk
www.simonandschuster.com.au

For my brother, Roger.
And for Maggie,
for opening all the doors.

1
My girl

For what is a brat, what has he got
When he finds out that he cannot
Say the things he truly thinks
But only words, not what he feels

'My Way'
Sex Pistols

The first time I saw her was at my dad's funeral.

I know what you're thinking – his dad dies of cancer and a few days later he's eyeing up some girl.

It wasn't like that.

Well. It was. But it's not like I was on the pull or anything. And it wasn't as if I could see much of her, either. She was wearing an enormous overcoat. Just a flash of blonde hair showing over the top.

I didn't notice her at first.

I was sitting there, front row of the crematorium,

1

between Mum and Chloe. I knew the place was packed –
I'd turned round a few times and had a look. Lots of black
clothes and pale faces. It was January – dead cold, with ice
on the roads, so Mum was worried people wouldn't turn up.
But they did – masses of them. All Dad's family. Friends.
Even a couple of ex-girlfriends who made a big show of
coming up to Mum, arms outstretched, trying to hug her.

Mum was hating it. I could hear her teeth grinding. And
she was gripping my arm tight with her fingers.

Then Uncle Matt stepped up to the front. He's not my real
uncle, just Dad's best mate. The crematorium went quiet.

Uncle Matt talked about Dad – how he'd known him
since they were at school. How my dad was this great guy.
Loved punk music. Played the guitar when he was
younger. Always in trouble as a kid. *Blah, blah.* Loads of
laughs. *Blah, blah.* Spirit of adventure.

I'd heard it all before and it still didn't make sense. I
mean, Uncle Matt was making out like Dad was this real
rebel when he was young. But *real* rebels don't give it all
up for a nine-to-five job and a mortgage.

No way.

Not that Dad couldn't be a laugh sometimes. But he was
ordinary. Just an ordinary, middle-aged guy with an ordinary, boring, office job.

"But in those last few weeks," Uncle Matt went on,

"what he told me he would miss most of all was the chance to see his children grow up."

Mum's grip on my arm tightened even further. I could hear lots of sniffing behind me. I glanced sideways at Chloe. Tears were streaming down her face. She was always closer to Dad than me. I mean, it's not like Dad and I had lots of rows or anything. But he'd been ill for so long. And we'd never had much in common. I don't think he had any idea who I was.

Maybe that's why I didn't feel like crying. Maybe that's why his dying didn't feel real.

Uncle Matt sat down and a couple more people stood up. Someone read a poem. After that Chloe started bawling loudly and Mum leaned right across me to hold her hand. I wanted to get up and switch seats but it would have been too embarrassing. So we all stayed there, in what must have looked like this massive, miserable cuddle.

At last it was over. At the end they played "My Way". Not the classic Frank Sinatra everyone's heard of – but this punk version. Apparently Uncle Matt reckoned my dad would've loved it.

It just sounded stupid.

Getting out of the crematorium building took ages. Mum was still clutching my arm, stopping as person after person came up to her.

". . . so sorry . . ."

". . . a release . . ."

". . . miss him so much . . ."

As we reached the door I caught sight of Chloe. She was standing near all the flowers laid out on the ground, surrounded by girls from her class.

I recognised most of her friends. Chloe's a year older than me but we get on quite well. So long as I stay out of her room she's pretty cool. Anyway, right now she and her friends were all crying their eyes out. The other girls were hugging her and patting her on the shoulder, each of them jostling for the position of Most Important Friend at the Funeral.

All except her. The girl in the enormous overcoat.

She was standing slightly on the edge of the group. I was sure I hadn't seen her before, even though at that point I could only see her big coat and the back of her head. I stared at the way her smooth blonde hair curled onto her back.

And then she turned round.

I couldn't move. I couldn't breathe. I just stood, transfixed by her face.

She was beautiful.

Not attractive. Not pretty.

Massively, awesomely beautiful. Like a model or a film

star. Heart-shaped face. Big eyes. And these incredibly sexy, pouty lips.

I'd never seen a real person who looked that good.

"Luke," Mum hissed.

"What?" I said.

"Uncle Matt was just speaking to you. Why didn't you say something?"

I shook my head. I was dying to look at the girl again. I hadn't even heard Uncle Matt.

"Can I go and see if my mates are here?" I said.

Mum sighed. "Of course," she said. "But don't go far away. I . . . I . . ." Her voice cracked and she looked down.

I felt a stab of guilt as she let go of my arm. But Uncle Matt was instantly at her side, taking her hand and drawing her over to talk to some other people. I sighed with relief. Then turned round to look for the girl.

She was still there. I wanted to see what she looked like under that huge black overcoat. It was way, way too big for her. The shoulders hung halfway down her arms and the sleeves dangled below her hands.

With a jolt I realised it was a man's coat. It was January. It was cold. Somebody must've lent it to her to keep her warm. *Let it be her father*, I prayed. *Or her brother. Please.*

One of Mum's friends came up to me, clucking about

how sad it was that Dad had died, asking how I was coping. I answered in grunts, hoping she'd get the message and leave me alone. I still hadn't seen anyone from my class. I knew some of them were here. They were probably too embarrassed to come and speak to me after all Chloe's noisy crying in the service.

Chloe was blowing her nose now. The skin around her eyes was red and streaks of make-up were smeared down her cheeks. She was talking to the girl in the big overcoat. My girl.

I was thinking about going a bit closer. Chloe was my sister, after all – surely it wouldn't look too obvious?

And then this guy wandered over to them. He was tall. Older. I vaguely recognised him as a sixth-former from school. He said something to Chloe, then slipped his arm round the girl. My heart beat faster. I mentally measured the overcoat against his broad shoulders. *Bastard*. It was his coat. Had to be. *Please let him be her brother*.

It was my one remaining hope. Then the girl looked up, gave him this dead sexy grin, and my hope was dashed.

2

The records

Is she really going out with him?
Is she really gonna take him home tonight?
Is she really going out with him?
'Cause if my eyes don't deceive me
There's something going wrong around here.

'Is She Really Going Out With Him?'
Joe Jackson

The girl didn't come back to our house. Neither did her boyfriend. I tried not to imagine what they might be doing instead.

The house was full of the family and friends who'd been at the funeral. The women brought food and laid it out on the kitchen table. The men produced bottles of whisky and made whisky sours. I hovered, hoping one of them would offer me a glass.

They didn't.

Mum and Chloe stood in the living room, surrounded by people. I kept looking at the armchair Dad used to sit in all day before he had to go into the hospice. It felt odd seeing other people sprawled all over it.

None of my mates had made it back from the crematorium. I guessed they'd gone off to the park to play football. I didn't blame them really. In fact I was pulling on my trainers in order to join them, when Uncle Matt cornered me in the hall.

"Where're you going?" he said. I could smell the faint tang of whisky on his breath.

"Just out." I stood up.

Uncle Matt put his beefy hand on my shoulder. "Look, son," he said. "I know this is hard on you, but how's your mum going to feel if you clear off now?"

I gritted my teeth. "I'm not your son," I muttered.

Uncle Matt's already flushed cheeks reddened further. His hand dropped from my shoulder. "No, I didn't mean . . ."

"Luke?" Mum appeared behind him. She was smiling, but her eyes had this awful, dead look about them. "Are you feeling all right?" she said.

"I just want to be on my own for a while." I looked at the hall carpet.

"Course," she said. "You go out, get some air."

*

I came back an hour later. I hadn't gone to the park in the end, just walked around a bit. When it came down to it, I couldn't face seeing my friends. Since Dad had got ill, they'd all been a bit weird with me – like they didn't know what to say to me anymore.

I didn't need that – especially today.

The house was virtually empty now. A couple of Mum's friends were still there, collecting up empty bottles and sweeping plastic cups and bits of sandwich crust into black bin bags. They told me Mum was upstairs, lying down.

But it wasn't Mum I wanted to see. While I'd been out walking I couldn't stop thinking about the girl from the funeral. I kept looking out, hoping I'd bump into her. But, of course, I didn't.

I had to know who she was. I went upstairs and knocked on Chloe's bedroom door – she's liable to go mental if you don't knock and wait for a reply.

"Go away," said a teary voice.

I pushed the door open a fraction. Chloe was sitting on her bed, surrounded by photographs. She looked up at me, wiping her face and scowling. "What d'you want?"

I hesitated. In this mood, Chloe was unlikely to tell me anything. I'd probably be better off waiting until later.

"Just wanted to see if you were OK," I lied.

Chloe narrowed her eyes. "Yeah, right," she said. "By

the way, thanks for pigging off earlier and leaving me to cope with Mum on my own."

It was clearly hopeless. I closed the door and turned away, but to my surprise Chloe called after me. "Hey, Luke, come back."

I opened the door again. Chloe stared at me for a second, then beckoned me over to the bed.

"D'you wanna look at these old photos of Dad?" She pointed to the snaps spread out on the duvet in front of her.

Not for the first time I marvelled at how quickly her moods could change. I tried not to step on any of the clothes and magazines littering Chloe's carpet as I crossed the room. I knelt down beside the bed and bent over the pictures.

Most were of Dad on his own, but there were some with Chloe in as well. She pointed to one where Dad was giving her a piggyback ride. She looked about six or seven. They were both laughing.

"So how was it for you?" I said. "The funeral and stuff?"

Chloe made a face. "Gross."

"At least all your friends turned up," I said, hoping my attempt to edge the conversation to the girl wouldn't look too obvious.

"Yeah but half of them were only there 'cause they got

the morning off school," Chloe said. She picked up the picture of her and Dad and stared at it.

I seized my opportunity.

"Yeah, like, there was one girl I've never even seen before," I said. "Blonde. Wearing this outsize overcoat?"

Chloe put down the photo. "You mean Eve? She's OK, actually. Only started this term."

"In your class?" I said, casually.

Chloe nodded.

That meant Eve must be sixteen, or nearly sixteen. Whichever – she was a whole school year above me.

"She was dead sweet when she found out about Dad," Chloe went on, "though I wouldn't have asked her to the funeral if I'd known she was going to bring her boyfriend."

"Oh?" I said innocently. "She's got a boyfriend already?"

"Only the hottest guy in his year. Ben – he plays for City Juniors."

"Oh."

There was a knock at the door. Without waiting for Chloe to reply, Mum walked in, carrying a cardboard box. A large, bulky envelope was balanced on top of the box.

"Oh good, you're both here," Mum said, sitting down on the end of the bed.

I glanced at Chloe, wondering if she was going to flip into a mood at Mum for barging in like that. But Chloe was staring at the box and the envelope. "What are they?" she said.

Mum pressed her lips together. Long pause. I started thinking about the girl again. Eve. It was the perfect name for her. Simple and sexy. The overcoat she'd been wearing kept pushing its way into my mind's eye. Her supposedly "hot" boyfriend's coat. How come he got to have her? Sometimes life really sucked.

"Luke?"

I focused on Mum. She was frowning gently at me.

I felt myself going red. "Sorry," I muttered. "What did you say?"

Mum sighed. I was suddenly aware of how tired she looked. "Dad left this for you." She pushed the cardboard box she'd been holding across the bed to me. I stared down at it, blinking hard.

"For me?" I said.

"Yeah, doof brain. For you." Chloe was next to me, the bulky envelope that Mum had been carrying in her lap. She pointed to it. "I got a letter."

"Dad started trying to write to you too, Luke," Mum said quickly. She tapped the lid of the box. "But in the end he thought what's in there might be more meaningful right now." She paused. "Everything you need for them is up in the loft. If you can't set it up, Uncle Matt said he'd do it for you."

"I'm sure I'll be able to manage." I stood up. I had no idea what was inside the box, but the last thing I wanted was Uncle Matt muscling in with his *now, son, do it like this* routine.

I carried the box back to my bedroom and pushed open the door with my feet.

I sat down on the bed, the cardboard box on my lap. What on earth was inside that Dad thought was so meaningful?

I lifted the lid. Inside the box was a row of twenty or so paper envelopes with black discs inside. I pulled one out. Then another. They were vinyl records. Old ones. The paper sleeves were all scuffed and dirty. I recognised less than half of the bands. Not surprising. The tracks were all dated from ages ago – the late Seventies and early Eighties.

These were Dad's old singles. Records from when he was a teenager. My heart beat faster, and for the first time that day a huge sob rose up in my throat.

Was that all he thought of me?

Chloe gets a massive letter and I get palmed off with a bunch of ancient, crappy records. I pushed down the sob.

Dad wasn't worth crying over. I just had to accept it. He had no idea about my life.

No idea about me.

I put the box down on the floor and walked over to my window.

I wondered where Eve was. And what she was doing.

3

Meeting

Ever fallen in love with someone
Ever fallen in love
In love with someone
Ever fallen in love
In love with someone
You shouldn't've fallen in love with?

'Ever Fallen In Love?'
Buzzcocks

I couldn't wait to get back to school.

The funeral was on a Thursday, and Mum'd said Chloe and I could both have the next day at home if we wanted. She was surprised when I told her I'd rather be at school. Normally I'm up for any chance to get a day off.

It wasn't that I was hoping to see Eve. Well. Only a bit. Being at home was just too depressing. Mum cried all the time. Not loudly. Never even openly, but she wandered

15

around looking so sad it made me feel terrible. I tried to give her a hug a couple of times. But that just made her cry more. She always ended up pushing me away, saying something like: "I won't lay all this on you, Luke, it's not fair."

I wanted to say none of it was fair. But I didn't know how to say it. And I felt guilty that she was so unhappy and I hardly thought about Dad at all.

I hadn't played any of his old records. Mum had given me Dad's old-style record player out of the loft. I don't know why she'd thought I might need Uncle Matt's help to set it up. The thing was out of the dark ages, technology-wise – a switch for the record setting (45, 33 or 78), an on/off button and a volume knob.

I plugged it into the socket in the corner of my room, then covered it over with a towel. When Mum asked if I'd listened to any of Dad's records yet, I just said I wasn't ready and she let me alone.

In the end, being back at school wasn't much better than being at home. My friends were all dead weird with me. It was like they didn't know what to say to me about Dad, so they'd decided it was easier not to say anything. It's hard to explain. They talked and joked like always and we played football just as before, but there was this way they had of looking at me, like I came from another planet and might mutate into a bloodsucking alien at any minute.

I wasn't Luke anymore. I was the bloke with the Dead Dad.

And then there was Eve. Or, rather, there wasn't. That first day I looked out for her all the way to school, then again when I was leaving. No sign. I even walked past Chloe's classroom once – but it was empty.

That was Friday. The weekend passed slowly. By Monday I'd almost convinced myself I'd imagined her. Certainly I must have imagined how beautiful her face was. And I hadn't even seen the rest of her.

Chloe and I hardly ever walked to school together, but we sometimes met up to come home. That Monday afternoon I was hanging about by the wall near the entrance gates, half waiting for her. It was in the back of my mind that when Chloe came out with the rest of her class, Eve might be there too. But I wasn't really thinking about it.

I looked up. There was Chloe, surrounded by her friends as usual. They were giggling. Looking at their mobiles. A few of them wandered off. The rest shuffled round.

And I saw her.

She was smiling, listening to someone. My mouth fell open. She was even hotter than I'd remembered. I stared, trying to take all of her in at once. Long, slim legs. Curves everywhere. Sleek blonde hair falling dead straight onto her shoulders. And that face. *Jesus*. Even the way she stood was sexy. Her head to one side. Her hand, pushing back her jacket, resting on her hip.

The other girls drifted away. It was just her and Chloe now. Then they started walking across the tarmac. Except Eve didn't walk. The way she moved was more like gliding. Like a cat – smooth and fluid and unbelievably sure of herself.

Oh crap. They were coming towards me. They were wrapped up in their conversation, not looking at me, but they were definitely heading in my direction. Getting closer and closer. In a minute she was going to be standing right next to me. My heart pummelled against my ribs.

Seconds pulsed by. I stared down at the ground. And then she was here. Close enough to touch.

"Luke?" Chloe sounded impatient.

I looked up at my sister, catching Eve out of the corner of my eye. My throat was dry. Lust rocketed through me. There was nothing about her that wasn't perfect. The way her upper lip dipped into a V in the middle. The way her jumper clung to her . . .

"What the hell is wrong with you?" Chloe said.

I shook my head. "Nothing," I blurted out.

Stop. You're behaving like a total nutter. Calm down.

I looked down at the tarmac again. There was this tightness in my chest. It crossed my mind that I might be having a heart attack. I stood there, concentrating on breathing. Eve dragged one of her feet seductively across the tarmac. She was wearing black shoes with thin, pointy heels.

Chloe had clearly decided to ignore my peculiar behaviour. "So where're you meeting Ben?" she said to Eve.

"The Bell."

Oh God. Even her voice was sexy – all low and raspy.

"Ben's done me this new, totally brilliant fake I.D.," Eve said. "We're meeting for cocktails at happy hour."

Chloe giggled. "Oooh. Cocktails," she said.

"Yeah." I could hear the grin in Eve's voice. "Guess what his favourite is?" She leaned over and whispered something in Chloe's ear.

Chloe squealed. "No *way*. I can't believe they're even allowed to print that on a menu."

"They're not – but Ben knows the barman. They make it up for him specially."

I decided that I hated Ben.

"Anyway, I'd better go home and get ready," Eve said. "Bye, Chloe." She turned slightly sideways. I could tell she was looking at me. "Bye," she said.

I had to say something. I might not get this close to her

19

again for days. I looked up. Eve was smiling at me, her lips slightly parted.

I stared at her mouth, feeling my face redden. "Bye," I squeaked.

For God's sake, look at her properly.

I forced myself to look her straight in the eyes. They were almond-shaped, the palest blue I'd ever seen. But I could tell she wasn't really seeing me. Like, she was right there, looking in my direction, but not . . . not noticing me.

And then she was gone. As she glided through the school gates, Chloe swung her bag over her shoulder.

"Did you have to behave like that?" she snapped.

I swallowed. How much had she noticed? "What d'you mean?"

"Hardly looking up at Eve, like that. Not saying anything. It was really rude."

My mouth fell open, but Chloe had already stomped off towards the gates.

Over the next few days I seemed to see Eve everywhere – wandering down the corridor, chatting with her friends in the cafeteria, smiling mysteriously on her mobile.

I dreamed of going up to her, but I didn't have the nerve. Even if Eve didn't think I was rude – or a complete retard – I had no idea what to say to her. So I watched her from a distance.

If you're thinking that seeing her must have got easier, let me tell you – it didn't. Every time was like the first time.

A slap in the face. A punch in the stomach. A kick in the head.

She was the hottest person I'd ever met. But she had a boyfriend. And, even if she didn't, what chance would I have had with her? No girl I knew had ever gone out with a boy in a lower year.

I talked to other girls. I did my homework. I played football. I even spent a couple of hours looking through Dad's singles collection, though I didn't actually play any of the records. Part of me wanted to, but it was like, if I listened to them, I'd be saying everything between me and Dad was OK. That I forgave him for leaving me such a useless, heartless pile of crap.

Nothing took my mind off Eve.

February began. It was a cold day – exactly a month since Dad died, or so Mum said. Still dark when I got home from school. I'd been in my room. Then I got hungry and came down to the kitchen. As I reached the door, I overheard Mum on the phone.

"It's just so hard to tell," she was saying. "He's so with-drawn, just stays in his room all the time. Only comes out for meals."

Was she talking about me?

"OK, OK, I'll ask them," Mum said. "I'll let you know."

She hung up the phone, then called me and Chloe into the kitchen.

We sat down at the table. Chloe's face was covered in green gunk – some kind of face mask. A few weeks ago I would have made some jokey comment about how hideous she looked – or at least tried to make her laugh so that the dried mask cracked. But now, I couldn't be bothered. My head was too full of Eve.

"A group of us – girlfriends – want me to go away with them to this spa," Mum said nervously. "Just for one night. A week on Saturday. I said I would ask you, see what you both thought."

I tried to look interested.

Chloe's eyes widened. "You mean leave us on our own?"

Mum bit her lip. "I thought maybe you could both organise sleepovers but if—"

"No way." Chloe thumped her fist on the table. "I'm six-teen! I'm perfectly capable of staying here overnight by myself. Send Luke off to a friend, but I won't go."

"Hey," I said indignantly. "If she's staying, so am I."

Mum looked at us both as if she was trying to make up her mind.

"You should go, Mum." Chloe's voice was suddenly soft and gentle. "You deserve a break. And you don't need to worry about us. I'll look after Luke."

I opened my mouth to protest that I didn't need looking after, but Chloe glared at me. I shut up. Whatever. What did it matter really?

I would have taken a lot more interest if I'd known what Chloe was planning – and where it would lead.

4
The party

I said 'I'll see you later'
and I give her some old chat.
But it's not like that on the TV when it's
cool for cats.

'Cool For Cats'
Squeeze

Mum ran through the arrangements for what felt like the millionth time. "Uncle Matt's going to stop by at nine – just to make sure you're OK. Then I'll call before I go to bed – probably about eleven. Any problems call Matt or go down to the Wilsons at number forty-five. And for God's sake, Chloe, remember to lock up at night. Two twists on the Chubb and don't open the door unless you're sure who it is."

I glanced at Chloe. She was taking all the fuss remarkably well, considering how moody she normally was. I guess she didn't want any last-minute arguments stopping Mum from going.

Mum picked up her overnight bag and took two steps closer to the front door.

"Now, Luke, Chloe's in charge for tonight. Whatever she tells you to do, you do."

I shrugged. "Sure." *Well that should get me nicely off the hook if Mum ever finds out about tonight.*

Mum took another step across the hall, then clutched her forehead. "Oh no." She dropped her bag.

"What?" Chloe said, with just the barest trace of impatience.

"I haven't shown you where the stopcock for the water is. Or the fuse box."

" 'S'OK, Mum," I said. "I know. Dad showed me."

She smiled sadly at me, then picked up her bag. "Are you really sure about this, you two?"

"Yes."

"Course, Mum." I leaned forwards and kissed her on the cheek. "Have a good time."

As the door closed behind her, Chloe punched the air.

"Yesss!" she hissed. "Now, come on. We haven't got long to get ready."

Chloe had worked on Mum for two days to convince her we'd be all right on our own. The reason was obvious –

but Mum never guessed. We were going to have a party.

It was Chloe's thing really. She'd gone a bit mad since Dad died, going out all the time; pushing it with Mum in a way she never used to. I overheard her talking about the party to one of her friends, saying it was just what she needed to get her mind off Dad.

Maybe.

I'd mentioned it to a couple of mates, but to be honest, I wasn't all that excited about the party itself. Only in whether Eve would turn up.

My heart raced whenever I thought about it.

Eve. Here in my house.

And her boyfriend, said an annoying voice in my head.

I told it to shut up.

"Luke, are you listening to me?" Chloe shook my arm.

"Yeah, right," I said, quickly. "Tell me again."

"I need you down here to open the door when people bring stuff round this afternoon."

I screwed up my face. "Where are you going, then?" I said.

Chloe rolled her eyes. "I told you. I've got to get ready."

Chloe's idea of getting ready meant spending three hours on the phone to her friends discussing the clothes they were going to wear and the boys they wanted to get off with – and then soaking in the bath for an hour.

During the afternoon I let in a number of blokes – most of them from Chloe's class – each of them delivering a bottle of wine or vodka that they'd nicked out of their parents' cupboards. They all asked to see Chloe, but with every arrival she'd just drift out into the landing, phone firmly clamped in her hand, wave down at them, then drift away again.

Three of Chloe's girlfriends arrived at about six. They were all carrying armfuls of clothes and an assortment of bags and boxes. They vanished into Chloe's bedroom, where loud squeals soon rose up over the music.

I stayed downstairs, wondering what the hell they were doing. I'd already cleaned my teeth, dragged a clean T-shirt over my head and used some deodorant. It had taken five minutes. Even allowing for putting on make-up, how much more was there to getting ready than that?

At half-past eight Chloe appeared in the kitchen.

I stared at her. She was wearing masses of make-up, an ultra-tight top and a skirt that barely covered her bum. She smiled distractedly at me, then crossed the room to the fridge and pulled open the door.

"Dad would hate you looking like that." The words were out of my mouth before I'd even realised I was going to say them.

Chloe whipped round, whatever she had wanted from the fridge forgotten. "Yeah, well, he's not here is he?"

We glared at each other. For a second Chloe's bottom lip trembled. "You bastard," she said. She raced out of the room.

I sat there, feeling uncomfortable. When Chloe's angry with you, pretty much anything can happen. But to my surprise, when she reappeared fifteen minutes later she was wearing a big cardigan over the tight top, and had wiped some of the make-up off her face. She even had on a slightly longer skirt.

"This isn't 'cause of what you said," she said haughtily. "It's 'cause Matt'll be here in a minute."

"Right," I said. But I noticed, after Matt had been and gone, that although Chloe took off the cardigan, she didn't change back into the shorter skirt. Or, as far as I could tell, put on more make-up.

Mum phoned in at eleven. Chloe was all prepared for the call. She'd waited in her room for five minutes, telephone in hand.

When she reappeared to tell me I could stop fending people off the volume dial on her MP3 player she had a broad grin on her face.

"Nothing to worry about now," she said, turning the music back up.

I wasn't so sure.

For a start, there were already masses of people in the house. And more kept coming. Not just people from my year and Chloe's, but quite a lot of the sixth form and a few others I didn't recognise at all. Older blokes with high-heeled girls hanging off one arm and six-packs of beer in the other.

Somebody brought in this massive sound system and, minutes later, the deep bass of the music was making the whole house vibrate. It seemed to give the party this new dimension – darker and rougher. By midnight, most of the people from my year had disappeared and I'd lost sight of Chloe completely.

Eve arrived at eight minutes past midnight. She was wearing jeans with this white top that curled tantalisingly across her belly button. Unlike most of the other girls, she had hardly any make-up on. She didn't need it. She was better-looking than everyone else at the party put together.

Her boyfriend had his arm clamped round her waist, as if daring anyone to try and take her away from him. I hadn't seen him up close since the funeral. He wasn't that attractive, I decided. His nose looked broken and he had a fat neck.

Anyway, he and Eve wandered into the living room. I followed. They stood in a corner and started snogging almost immediately.

I watched, hating it. Hating him. Rage surged up from my stomach, bitter in my mouth. I turned away, so full up with anger I didn't know what to do with myself. It wasn't just the stupid boyfriend either. I was furious with Eve for liking him. And with Chloe for letting the party get so out of hand. Who *were* all these people?

But, most of all, I was angry with myself for letting it all get to me. This was a party, for goodness sake. Why couldn't I just chill? Get into the whole thing.

I looked round. There were loads of girls here on their own. And some of them were really hot. Not Eve-hot. But good enough.

Gritting my teeth, I marched through the dancing bodies that filled our living room, to a short, pretty girl with dark hair who was standing beside the light switch. I'd noticed her dancing with at least four different guys earlier. Now she looked bored.

This made me hopeful.

"Hi," I said. "What's your name?"

She stared at me. "Why?"

I shrugged, my nerve failing fast. "Wanna dance?"

The girl gave me a withering look. "With you?" she said.

I nodded, feeling my face and neck flushing red. The girl stared at me for several, long seconds.

"You have to be kidding," she said. Then she stalked off towards the kitchen.

With a sigh I turned round and leaned against the wall. Humiliation now mingled with my anger. Why was it so hard? How did all these other guys do it?

I glanced over at Eve and Ben. They were sitting in Dad's old armchair now, still snogging furiously. As I watched them, despair flooded through me. Ben's hands were trying to get under Eve's white top. She was pushing them away, but he got rougher, more insistent.

Why didn't she just stop kissing him?

I clenched my fists and left the room.

I stomped upstairs. There were couples everywhere. On the steps, on the landing, in the bathroom.

I sat on the top step of the stairs and put my head in my hands.

A minute later I felt the step below me creak. For one glorious fantastical moment I imagined it might be Eve. I looked up. Ryan Kennedy – a boy I knew vaguely from the parallel class in my year – was standing in front of me. He had a wide mouth, dark, floppy hair and – I was pretty sure – had arrived at the party with lots of friends of both sexes.

"Hi." He smiled.

"Hi," I said, grumpily, hoping he would go away.

"I saw you downstairs," Ryan said, sitting down next to me. "I know what you want."

I stared at him. For a single, horrified second I wondered if he was hitting on me. Then I remembered seeing him earlier, dancing with the short, pretty brunette who'd just blown me off.

This didn't make me feel any better.

"What are you talking about?"

Ryan lowered his voice, so I could only just hear him above the thump of the music. "Eve. Eve Ripley, the new girl in your sister's class."

I shrugged. "Dunno what you mean."

"Yeah, right," Ryan's smile broadened. "It's written all over your face. Like I said, man. I was watching you downstairs."

I glared at him. "Why don't you piss off?"

Ryan appeared to take this as an invitation to stretch out his legs. We sat in silence, watching a girl in a pair of high-heeled boots tottering towards us up the stairs. As she pushed her way past, she giggled.

"Hi, Ry," she said. "See you later?"

Ryan grinned up at her. "Maybe."

The girl giggled again and stumbled off towards the bathroom.

I leaned forwards, intending to get up and go and shut myself in my bedroom.

32

"Hey." Ryan's hand on my shoulder pulled me back. "Don't you wanna know how I can help you get her?" he said. "Eve, I mean."

"No," I snapped, shaking off his hand. "Funnily enough, I'm not in the mood for a humiliating wind-up."

"OK." He shrugged. "Your choice. But it's not a wind-up. It really works."

I frowned, curious in spite of myself. "What works?"

Ryan gave me a lazy, lopsided grin. "The Six Steps. They're these steps you gotta follow. Get you any girl you want."

"What?" I said.

"Six Steps, man. Like a list of things you've got to do."

He had to be kidding me.

"What d'you mean?"

But Ryan was looking down the stairs again, waving.

A girl in a short skirt with a tumble of red curls was standing on the bottom step, smiling up at us. She was strikingly pretty. Not like Eve, of course. But still . . .

The girl waved, then tapped her watch. Ryan stood up. "Look, man, I gotta leave now. I'll tell you about the Six Steps later, OK?"

I looked up. Ryan's face was open, his eyes serious. Something told me that he meant what he was saying. That, for some reason, he really wanted to help me.

"I don't—?"

"I'll talk to you Monday – explain it all then."

"Right," I said, sinking back against the banisters, determined to look uninterested. "Whatever."

Ryan grinned, then he slipped down the stairs and took the girl's hand. I watched them weave their way towards the front door.

The music was even louder now. The bass pounded up through the floorboards, vibrating against my feet. I got up and wandered across to the landing window that looked over the front of the house.

Ryan and the girl were disappearing up the road. As they reached the corner Ryan stopped and pulled her into this massive snog.

I leaned my forehead against the cold window pane. Ryan wasn't any older or better-looking than me. And yet he had girl after girl practically throwing themselves at him. What did he know that I didn't?

I kicked the wall at my foot.

Without looking up from the girl, Ryan lifted one arm and waved lazily back at the house.

5

First steps

'Cause I'm gonna make you see
There's nobody else here.
No one like me.
I'm special . . . so special.
I gotta have some of your attention.
Give it to me.

'Brass In Pocket'
Pretenders

The living room was a total mess. Torn plastic cups, over-flowing ashtrays and empty beer cans lay everywhere. All Mum's CDs were on the floor. Three cushions were ripped and there were several dark stains on the sofas and carpet.

"After everything your mum's been through this year," Uncle Matt roared. "All she wanted was a little time to her-self. And now she's got to come home to this."

"We'll clear up in the morning," Chloe slurred.

She looked totally wrecked. Her make-up was all smeared and her tight top was twisted so far round that it was almost back to front.

"No way, madam," Uncle Matt snapped. "You're clearing up now."

It was one a.m. Shortly after Ryan had left, the police had turned up, investigating complaints about noise from the neighbours. When they realised how young Chloe was they turned off the music and made everyone leave.

They wanted to call Mum, but Chloe begged them not to. In the end they compromised on Uncle Matt, after we explained he was the family friend who'd been left in charge while Mum was away. Matt turned up shortly afterwards – furious with both of us.

He made us work until three a.m. My job was to go round the house getting all the wine and beer stains off the floor and furniture. I used a whole bottle of stain remover, pretending each dirty mark that I scrubbed was Ben's face. What a jerk. I couldn't get the image of him groping Eve on Dad's armchair out of my head. What the hell did she see in him?

Matt let us sleep until seven, then woke us again so we could open all the windows and vacuum before Mum got home. I can't tell you how annoying it was to have him bossing us around in our own house, but we kept our mouths shut – hoping that, if we did everything he told us, he wouldn't tell Mum what had happened.

I don't know what fantasy land we were living in.

To be fair, Matt played down the whole thing in terms of how trashed the house had been. But for Mum, the very fact that we'd lied to her was the worst thing.

"I'm so disappointed in you both," she said. "And Dad would've been too."

I'd rather she'd shouted at us.

In the end, Chloe was grounded for a month for organising the party and I was grounded for a week for not grassing her up. Neither of us thought this was particularly fair, and the rest of the weekend passed in an atmosphere of slammed doors and long, dark silences.

I didn't see Eve on Monday. But Ryan sauntered up to me while I was choosing a lunchtime sandwich in the school cafeteria.

"So," he said, balancing his tray in one hand. "Six Steps. You interested?"

I glanced round. No one else was within earshot.

"I don't get it," I hissed. "Why d'you want to help me?"

"Lots of reasons." Ryan shrugged. "I told you. I've been there. Planet Hopeless. I just want to help."

I stared at him, still unconvinced.

"Look, man. I promise you I am not winding you up. Let's meet after school. I'll prove it."

"Can't. I'm grounded." I wasn't sure whether I felt more relieved or disappointed.

Ryan didn't look surprised. "We'll come to you, then," he said.

"We?" I said. "Who's 'we'?"

But Ryan had already darted off into the crowds.

I felt anxious for the rest of the day. What was Ryan planning? Who was he going to bring with him? I wished I'd told him to get lost, straight out, when I'd had the chance.

He turned up about an hour after Chloe and I got home from school. My stomach twisted uncomfortably as I opened the door.

Ryan was with two other boys from his class. A skinny, red-haired geek with glasses known – for some reason – as Numbers, and a lumbering, acne-ridden giant called Tony. They didn't look like the sort of people Ryan usually hung out with.

"Hi Luke," Ryan said cheerily. "I brought a couple of mates with me. Hope that's OK. These two already know about the Six Steps. Numbers is here to boast. Tones is here 'cause I asked him and he owes me."

I could feel my face reddening. He hadn't said anything to them about me and Eve, had he? "I don't—"

"Don't worry – they don't know any details," Ryan said. "So, can we come in?"

Part of me wanted to shut the door in his face. But, though I hated to admit it, I was curious. I decided I'd listen to whatever Ryan's six stupid steps were – then chuck him and his loser friends out.

"OK," I said. "But I haven't got much time."

I led them into the living room. Ryan immediately sprawled across one of the sofas. "The first thing you should know," he said, "is that I know what I'm talking about. I've had more hot girls than anyone else in our year."

"Except me," Numbers said proudly.

I stared at him. Numbers was, frankly, scrawny. And he looked about eleven. There was no way he'd ever even held hands with a girl.

"I don't think so." Ryan turned to me. "Unlike Numbers here, I go for quality as well as quantity. Premiership babes only, like Kelly Simmonds and Jade Aziki."

My mouth fell open. Kelly and Jade were the best-looking girls in Ryan's class. No one I knew had come close to even getting a snog off them.

"Look." Ryan produced a mobile from his pocket. He handed it to me. "Look at numbers six through to fifteen."

I clicked through the pictures. There was Ryan with his arms round a succession of girls. Not just Jade and Kelly, but all sorts of others too. Most of them not even at our school.

"It's sort of my business catalogue," Ryan said, modestly.

"This doesn't prove anything," I said, though privately I was impressed.

"I've snogged seventy-six girls since November third," Numbers smirked.

"All thanks to the Six Steps," Ryan added.

" 'S true," grunted Tony from Dad's armchair. "I done all the Steps except the last one. 'S changed my life."

I stared at him. Tony's face was like a pizza, so covered in spots there was hardly any clear skin visible underneath. If Ryan's stupid plan could help Tony get a girl, maybe there was something in it.

"Numbers. Tones," Ryan said briskly. "Give us a few minutes, would you?"

They went out of the room. Ryan leaned forwards, all serious. "OK, those guys couldn't pull Eve Ripley if they were the last males on earth. But you can, if you listen to me. Now, the first thing I need is a history," he said. "Who've you been out with? How long did it last? How far did you get?"

"I'm not telling you that." I could feel myself going red.

With anyone else I'd just have exaggerated my experiences. Enjoyed doing it, in fact. But something told me Ryan would know if I lied.

Ryan sighed. "If you're not prepared to be open with me, I can't help you."

My temper rose. "Who says I want your help? Coming here with your freak-show friends. I'm doing fine by myself."

Ryan leaned back on the sofa. He looked neither upset nor angry at my outburst. After a few moments he shook his head sorrowfully. "You really like her, don't you?"

The way he looked at me, it was like he could see right inside my head.

"Face it, man," Ryan said. "At the moment you don't stand a chance. Eve Ripley's total Premiership. Top of the Premiership, in fact. And she's already got a boyfriend."

"Yeah," I muttered. "Dunno what she sees in him."

"Well, Ben's a football star." Ryan pursed his lips, thoughtfully. "Plus he's older than she is, he's tall and good-looking and all her friends fancy him."

"Right." I looked down at the carpet.

"I saw you with that short brunette at your party an' I gotta tell you, your technique totally sucks. But I reckon with a bit of training you'd be fine. So, stop making out you can do all this alone, and spill."

There was a long pause.

In spite of my irritation there was something about Ryan I liked. He was so direct and he *was* offering to help me, apparently just because he felt sorry for me. But there was still no way I was going to humiliate myself by telling him the truth about what I suspected was, compared to his, a pretty limited set of experiences.

Ryan sighed again. "OK, let me guess," he said. "The longest you've ever been out with someone is three weeks. You've got off with, say, between twenty and thirty girls – none of them Premiership. And you've never gone the whole way. Am I right?"

I stared at him. "Way off," I lied.

"Yeah, right." Ryan grinned. "This is gonna work, man. I've got a good feeling about it."

He went to the door and called Tones and Numbers back in. "You don't mind, do you?" he said. "They could prob- ably both do with a refresher, not that Numbers would ever admit it."

I winced. If anyone at school found out I'd been taking dating tips in some kind of girly group session . . .

"I don't know," I said.

"Will you chill?" Ryan sounded exasperated. "Don't you think that if either of them were going to say anything to anyone, they'd have already told on each other?"

I shrugged uneasily, as Numbers and Tones came in and sat down.

"Step One," Ryan said. "Look good – Feel good."

I stared at him. "What?"

"The first thing you need is confidence," Ryan said. "And the easiest part of confidence is making the most of how you look. Tell me, what did you do to get ready for the party?"

I told him.

Tones gave a low chuckle.

"You should've ironed the shirt," Ryan said. "You looked a mess. And not in a good way."

"What? No one's gonna notice if my shirt's all neat and stuff."

"Maybe not, but they'll notice if you look like an old tramp. And you need a haircut too. Something shorter. It's all gotta look like you take a pride in your appearance, but you aren't obsessed with it. Also, more washing and clean clothes and less deodorant. You don't want to overdo anything – especially deodorant and hair gel. But washing's cool."

"I do wash." I glared at him.

"Sure," Ryan said. "I'm just saying. To be honest I don't think you've got any problems. Is there anything you'd like to change about your appearance? Like being taller, for instance?"

I thought about Eve's hulking boyfriend. "Maybe." I shrugged.

Numbers snorted. "Join the club."

"You're taller than she is, aren't you?" Ryan said.

I nodded. I was, by a few centimetres. But Ben was a whole head and a half taller than me.

"Well, then," Ryan went on. "You don't need to worry. And even if you weren't taller there are ways round it. Ask Numbers."

Numbers grinned. "Ry told me to only ever chat birds up sitting down. Works like a dream. Once they've experienced the Numbers magic touch they don't care how tall I am."

I smiled weakly at him.

"OK. Step Two," Ryan said. "Noticing. Get her to notice you. Then make sure she knows you've noticed her."

"How?" I said, meaning: *how, without making a total tit of myself like I did last time?*

"Get her on her own. Show her that you're interested in something she's interested in. Girls love that sensitive stuff. But don't go all gushy and girly about it. Just be friendly."

"How do I find out what she's interested in without talking to her?"

Ryan rolled his eyes. "Look on the noticeboards at

school. See if she's signed up for any after-school stuff. Ask your sister. But be subtle. You've gotta make it clear to her you're interested, but still look cool."

"I was stuck on that for weeks," Tones said glumly. "Ry made me practice on about fifty girls before he said I was ready for . . . for her . . ."

I wondered who the object of Tones's desire was and how he had possibly managed to get anywhere near her.

"Let's practise," Ryan said. "Look at me like you're interested."

"What?" I said. "No way."

Ryan tutted. "Don't be so uptight, man. This is where most guys fall down. They either get stuck on being friends or they go way over the top and frighten the girl off. It's important."

"Why do I have to do some stupid 'look'? Can't I just go up to her and ask her out?" I said.

"No," Ryan said. "It's gotta be a look first, or you've blown it before you've begun. Come on. Numbers cracked this first time."

Stung, I tried to look at him as if I fancied him. It was impossible. Ryan was studying my face intently, like I was a bug under a microscope. "Give me more," he said.

"Jesus," I muttered. I tried to pretend I was looking at Eve and telling her with my eyes how much I liked her.

"Whoa." Ryan drew back in mock-horror. "Psycho alert. If you look at her like that she'll think you're some kind of stalker."

I felt my whole face flush with humiliation. "Well you do it if you're so clever," I said.

Ryan cocked his head on one side. "OK" He darted out of the living room, then reappeared about a minute later, Chloe's school bag in his hand. "She's looking for her homework," he grinned. "Should be in in a moment."

I glared at him. "You're not practising on my sister."

"Chill," Ryan said. "It's only a look, remember?"

I sat there, feeling uneasy. A few minutes later Chloe barged into the living room. She saw her bag where Ryan had put it, on the table in the corner, and stomped towards it. "What the hell is this doing here?" she muttered.

As she reached the table, Ryan sprang up and sauntered towards her. "Hi," he said. "Chloe, isn't it?"

Chloe glanced at him. I grinned. She was clearly in a foul mood. And the way she looked at Ryan was exactly the same as the way Eve had looked at me – a sort of looking through you, like you weren't really there.

"I'm sorry about your dad," Ryan said. "My dad died too, well my stepdad. The first few months are really tough."

My stomach tightened. Was that true? Ryan hadn't mentioned a dead stepfather to me. For a second I had this

46

image of Dad standing exactly where Ryan was now, in the middle of the room. Laughing.

I pushed the memory away. Dad wasn't here. I didn't have to think about him.

Chloe was looking at Ryan properly now. "Oh," she said. "Er . . . thanks." She picked up her bag and walked over to the door.

Ryan jogged round behind her and got there first. He opened the door and pushed it back to let her pass. Now I could see his face, but not Chloe's. He stared at her as she walked towards him. A deep, flirty, mysterious stare that seemed to shut out everyone else in the room. Chloe stopped. Though I couldn't see her expression, she was obviously looking back at him. Ryan held her gaze for maybe just a couple of seconds, then smiled and looked away.

My heart pounded. I was sitting here, watching some stupid bloke hit on my sister for a joke. No. Worse. To teach me how to pull someone else. A wave of anger and humiliation flooded through me as Chloe scuttled out of the room. Ryan closed the door and looked round at me triumphantly. "See?" he said.

I was across the room in two strides. I grabbed him by the collar and shoved him against the wall.

"Don't ever mess with my sister again."

Ryan's eyes widened. "Hey, man, you *asked* me to show you. But, fine, I won't go near her ever again. OK?"

I let go of his collar. My hands were shaking.

Ryan took a step away from me and smoothed down his clothes. "Anyway," he said. "The thing is, did you get how it works? The important part is holding that last second or two. If the look's too short they won't see it. Too long and you'll look creepy."

"Was any of that true, Ry?" Numbers said. "'Bout your stepdad?"

Ryan grinned. "Well, the last one left two years ago and I haven't seen him since, so he might as well be dead." He glanced at me. "No offence, man."

I looked away. It didn't matter to me what Ryan said.

" 'S genius," Tones grunted, mournfully. "Sheer chuffin' genius."

They left soon after. Ryan said two Steps was enough for one day.

I told him I thought his whole plan sucked, then I went upstairs and practised the "look" in the mirror for the rest of the night.

6

Collage materials

Picture this, a sky full of thunder.
Picture this, my telephone number.
One and one is what I'm telling you.
Oh yeah.

'Picture This'
Blondie

"Chloe, where should I get my hair cut?"

We were walking home from school the next day. Chloe looked at me suspiciously. "I thought you always went to that barber's in the high street. Where Dad used to go."

I shrugged. "Yeah. But it's full of old men and kids. I'm ready for something that'll make me look more . . . er . . . more . . ."

"More like a babe-magnet?" Chloe grinned. "Dream on."

I stopped. "If you're going to—"

"Hey, I'm just messing with ya," Chloe said. "Try Leather Stripes on the high street. Or Felloretti's."

"They sound like a strip joint and an ice-cream parlour," I said suspiciously.

Chloe laughed. "They're good places for blokes' hair. Most of Ben's year get their hair cut there."

"Right. Thanks." *Good. I love the way Ben comes up as a reference point for absolutely everything.*

Chloe teased me a bit more about why I wanted my hair cut. But she promised to cover for me with Mum as I was grounded and therefore supposed to go straight home from school.

I left her at the corner of the high street then went in search of Leather Stripes. It looked promising. Dark leather seats and wooden floors. And plenty of men inside getting their hair cut.

Half an hour later I emerged, transformed. The girl who'd done my hair had cut it quite flat on top with a short, spiky fringe. It looked good. I'd even got up the nerve to practise Ryan's 'look' on the hairstylist, though I'm not sure it worked very well. She offered me a glass of water and asked if I was feeling all right.

Finding out what Eve was interested in had turned out to be much easier than I'd expected. I already knew she was doing Art GCSE from things Chloe had said. And when I checked on the noticeboard her name was listed under the Year Ten and Eleven after-school Art Club, which met between four and five-thirty every Thursday. I signed up straight away.

Wednesday dragged by, then Thursday sped past like a bullet. Before I knew it, I was standing outside the art room at four p.m., pushing open the door, wondering if Eve was already there.

She wasn't. The room was almost empty: just a couple of girls in the corner going through a pile of drawings and the teacher – Ms Patel – a dumpy woman with long black hair down to her waist.

The art room was large and airy. It covered a quarter of the top floor of the school and had a long window running all the way down one side. There was a big teacher's desk at one end and four large wooden tables in the middle of the room. My heart leaped. Four tables meant a one-in-four chance Eve and I would sit at the same one.

The walls were covered with artwork. I wandered round, trying to spot Eve's name in the corner of any of the pictures.

"Hi, Luke, is it?" Ms Patel waddled over. "What's the project you're working on?"

My mouth went dry. *Stupid stupid stupid.* Why hadn't I

realised that if I joined an Art Club I'd have to do some art?

"Er . . . I don't have a project," I said. "I just wanted to try some stuff out."

Ms Patel frowned at me. "Well, most students here use the time to work on their GCSE coursework. But I know you're not taking Art GCSE. Which medium did you want to work in?"

I'll do whatever Eve's doing.

"Maybe I could just start off with some ordinary drawing," I stammered. "Then see what grabs me."

Ms Patel pursed her lips. "OK." She pointed to one corner. "Paper and charcoal over there. Watercolours by the sink. But I suggest you begin with pencil. Why don't you try sketching the vase of flowers on the window ledge."

She walked over to the long window, picked up a small white vase filled with some sort of large daisies, and plonked it on a table near the back of the room.

I gathered a sheet of paper and some satisfyingly sharp pencils and sat down. A few more people had come in by now. Only one boy, though, I noticed. Perhaps I should tell Numbers about Art Club. On second thoughts, I didn't need any more competition for Eve than I already had.

She arrived about ten minutes later. My heartbeat accelerated when I saw her. I looked quickly back down at my drawing. So far it looked more like an eggcup with alien heads growing out of it than a vase of flowers.

Eve sat down at the table at the back next to mine. She started chatting in a low voice to the two girls already sitting there. Out of the corner of my eye I watched a slick of sleek blonde hair fall sexily over her shoulder. It brushed across the edge of the bra strap that was peeking out from under her top. I closed my eyes and imagined rushing over, pushing the hair back and . . .

When I opened my eyes, her hair was tucked behind her ears and she was concentrating on the piece of paper in front of her. I squinted, trying to make out what she was working on, without staring too obviously.

It looked like she was sticking down bits and pieces of paper – a collage of some sort.

"How's it going, Luke?" Ms Patel's voice beside me made me jump.

"Er, not so good, Ms Patel," I said, honestly. "I don't think drawing's really my thing."

"Mmmn," she said. "Well, is there anything else you'd like to try?"

"I was thinking about doing a collage," I stammered.

"What of?"

Jesus. Ms Patel should get an award for asking difficult questions.

I stared helplessly round the room. My eyes lit on an old radio on the teacher's desk. "Music," I said. "I'd like to find some way of expressing the way music sounds in a picture. That's why collage is the perfect . . . er . . . er . . . medium."

"You mean because the sound is non-linear?" Ms Patel said. I had no idea what she was talking about, but I nodded anyway.

"Mmmn." Ms Patel nodded slowly. "I like it. The expression of the inexpressible. A disjointed refraction of the light within sound."

"Exactly," I said.

Ms Patel beamed at me.

"You need to decide on the kind of collage materials you want to use. I'll ask Eve if she can spare five minutes for a chat with you about the best options. She's doing a marvellous collage as part of her GCSE coursework."

I sat frozen to my seat. Eve was going to talk to me. Me. On my own. About collage materials, whatever they were.

There was no time to think. I heard Ms Patel talking, then the sound of a chair being scraped backwards across the floor. I looked up.

Oh God. She was right there. Right beside my table.

"Hi, I'm Eve." She slid into the seat next to me. My heart thumped. We were so close. If I moved my hand by a few centimetres it would touch hers.

"Luke," I said.

Eve was staring at my alien-head flowers.

"Just doodling," I said, scrunching the paper up in my hand.

She smiled at me. It was like someone shining a torch directly in my eyes. I had to look away.

"I remember you," she said. "You're Chloe's brother."

Yesss! Suddenly brimful with confidence, I looked back at her.

"I . . . er . . . I'm sorry about your dad." Eve blushed.

"It doesn't matter." *Shit.* "I mean . . . it's OK. Not him dy . . . I mean . . ." I tailed off.

Eve smiled again. "I like your music collage idea," she said. "Ms Patel said you wanted to know about the different materials you could use . . ."

"Mmmn," I said, nodding vaguely. "Mmmn." My eyes travelled slowly down her jumper, then back up to her mouth. I watched her lips, transfixed by the effortlessly sexy way they pouted and curled as she spoke.

". . . so paper's good, but messy. Maybe bottle tops would work – though they're hard to stick down. Or how about silver foil? That would get across the metallic quality of music, don't you think?"

It took me a couple of seconds to realise Eve had stopped talking and was now looking at me. I also realised, a heartbeat too late, that I was still staring at her mouth like some sex-crazed lunatic.

"Sorry if that was boring."

"No, it wasn't," I said, too quickly. "It was really helpful."

Crap, crap, crap. She thinks I'm being rude again.

Eve stood up. I stared at the tabletop, praying for inspiration. Something, anything to keep her here a minute longer.

"How about wood?" I said desperately. "Sorry if I went weird on you back there, but something you said made me think. The quality of music thing. I mean, metal's good – but so's wood, isn't it? After all, loads of instruments are made of wood."

I prayed Ms Patel wasn't about to appear at my shoulder and ask me which ones. At that point I don't think I could have named a single musical instrument, let alone worked out which ones were wooden.

Eve nodded. "I like it," she said. "Hey, why don't you use wooden buttons. That'll add to the whole effect by being disc-shaped. You know, like CDs?"

"That's brilliant," I said. "Thanks."

Eve looked pleased with herself. She walked back over to her table.

"OK, time to pack up," Ms Patel called.

I checked my watch. Where had the last half-hour gone?

My heart was racing as I replaced my pencils in the pencil box. Ms Patel cornered me before I could get back across the room. I explained the wooden-button collage idea as quickly as I could. I wanted to have time to say goodbye to Eve before she left.

"Great, but you'll have to bring in your own buttons next week," Ms Patel said. "We don't have any wooden ones."

"Fine." In the distance I could see Eve disappearing out the door. I almost skidded across the art-room floor to grab my bag, then raced onto the corridor. She was on her own, thank God, just at the top of the stairs.

"Eve," I called.

She looked up and smiled.

"See you next week," I said. My eyes lingered on her face. I wasn't even thinking about making her notice me or trying to look at her in any special way.

Then it happened. Without warning, this jolt – like an electric shock – shot between us. It was massive. Overpowering. Like . . . like in that instant we were inside each other's head and the rest of the world had disappeared. A second later it was gone.

I stared at her, knowing absolutely that she had felt it too.

Her face reddened. She looked away, clutching the stair rail.

"Next week," she said. Then she scurried off down the stairs.

I leaned against the wall, too turned on – too completely overwhelmed – to move. Then Ms Patel emerged from the art room and I dragged myself downstairs, sending a silent prayer of thanks to whoever, in their utter and total brilliance, had invented the wooden button.

7

Humiliation

And I thought I was mistaken
And I thought I heard you speak
Tell me how do I feel?
Tell me now how should I feel?

Now I stand here waiting.

'Blue Monday'
New Order

Ryan was impressed when I told him. "Fast work, man," he said. "You've cracked Step Two at the first attempt. Plus, that kind of vibe only happens when something real's going on."

We were in the high street, getting a lunchtime burger. It was the day after the after-school Art Club and I was still grinning like an idiot.

"Don't tell Numbers about it, though." Ryan leaned back in his chair and smiled. "He'll pester you for weeks to explain how you did it."

"I didn't 'do' anything," I said. "It just happened."

Ryan took a bite of his burger. "Yeah well, that's a bit subtle for Numbers. Remember all he wants is to get as far as he can, as quickly as he can, as often as he can. He's not fussy – he'd snog a lampost if it had tits and moved."

I laughed.

"Still, you gotta hand it to him – Numbers is brilliant at Step Three," Ryan said enigmatically. "Almost got a sixth sense about it."

I opened my mouth to ask what Step Three was, but at that moment the doors of the burger bar flew open and Ben strode in with a couple of his equally beefy, ugly mates. They sprawled across the large booth behind ours and yelled for the waitress. After she'd delivered their menus and they'd refused to move to a smaller table, they began boasting loudly at each other.

With a horrible, sinking sensation, I realised Ben must be talking about Eve.

". . . Yeah, we did that last night. She was all over me."

I froze, my burger halfway to my mouth.

"Stupid cow wouldn't go any further, though. So I told her I'd wait until she was sixteen for the actual shag." Ben laughed. "I made out I had no idea when that would be, that it didn't matter if it was months away, but really I knew and – get this – her birthday's in three weeks."

60

"Nice one," one of the other blokes said in a deep, gruff voice.

"Yeah." Ben was laughing so much now he was choking. "She was so grateful it was pathetic. All 'you're so amazing, Ben'; 'So sensitive to wait till I'm ready, Ben'." He said this in a high, silly falsetto as much unlike Eve's raspy voice as it could be.

My stomach twisted into this tearing, burning knot.

"After another fortnight she'll be gagging for it," Ben sneered. "Begging me to do her."

I put down my burger and looked up at Ryan. He was staring sympathetically at me.

His sympathy was the last thing I wanted.

"I'm not hungry," I said. I stumbled blindly out of the burger bar. Had I imagined the look that passed between me and Eve? No. And I certainly hadn't imagined her blushing. But maybe she hadn't felt it the same way I had. Maybe all I'd done was remind her of how she felt about her stupid thug of a boyfriend.

I fantasised about going back in the burger bar and punching Ben in the face. But I was too scared. He was much bigger than me. And he was with two friends.

Humiliated, I stomped off back to school.

Ryan turned up on the doorstep half an hour after Chloe

and I got home that evening. "Hey, Luke, man . . ." He gave me a pitying smile.

"Forget it." I started shutting the door in his face, hating that he felt sorry for me. "I'm not interested anymore."

Ryan shoved his foot in the gap and pushed against me. "Don't be so lame," he said. "You should be more determined than ever now."

"Oh yeah? How d'you work that out?"

"Because Ben's handed you Step Three on a plate, you idiot."

I opened the door. "What d'you mean?"

"I'm not telling you out here. Let me in."

Reluctantly, I led Ryan into the kitchen. Mum was out and Chloe was up in her room. I slumped into one of the kitchen chairs and drummed my fingers on the table. "Well?"

Ryan sat down. "You gotta have an Angle. That's Step Three. Some way of positioning yourself – like a brand in a shop. Some way of standing out from the crowd – a way that's particularly meaningful for whoever it is you're after."

I shook my head. Ryan talked as much rubbish as Ms Patel in the Art Club. "What the hell are you going on about?"

"Don't you see?" Ryan leaned forwards. "Ben's pushing Eve to go all the way with him."

I glared at him. "Thanks for the newsflash. I think I'd worked that out for myself."

"But she doesn't want to. Even you must have seen that."

"But Ben said—"

"What else was he gonna say, man? He was trying to look cool in front of his stupid mates."

"So how does that help me?" I said.

"Well, that's your Angle. If you wanna get her away from Ben, you've got to be the guy who doesn't push. The guy who's respectful. Maybe even a bit aloof."

I frowned. "So what you're saying is that the way to get her is to pretend I'm not interested."

"No." Ryan put his elbows on the table and lowered his head despairingly into his hands. "Why d'you have to make this such hard work? You make it clear you're interested, but you don't push. You let her come to you. It's perfect. After all, your biggest problem is coming across as this eager little kid. But with this Angle you're overcoming that *and* blowing Ben out of the water at the same time."

The doorbell rang. "That'll be Tones," Ryan said. "I invited him round for Step Four revision – it's his weakest point."

"Great," I said, sarcastically. "It's only my house. Invite who you like."

Ryan grinned. "Well I would have said come to mine, but you and your sister are still grounded, aren't you?"

The doorbell rang again.

"Are you getting that?" Chloe screeched from upstairs.

Step Four was Humour. Ryan was convinced that making a girl laugh got you halfway to everything else. "Of course," he said, pacing up and down the kitchen. "Numbers doesn't bother much with Steps Four onwards, but if you want to get someone hot you're gonna need something special."

Tones nodded seriously from the kitchen table. "I bin trying, Ry," he said. "D'you wanna hear this joke I learned?"

Ryan gazed at him fondly – rather like a mother duck might look at a particularly hopeless duckling. "Tones, we talked about this." He sighed. "Telling jokes is not your strong point. For you, it's gotta be low key. Like saying Mr Hedges has gotta face like a potato."

Tones grinned. "That's a good one. I'll remember that."

I shook my head as Ryan sat down beside Tones. A sense of humour wasn't something you could teach.

"Right, chat me up, Tones," Ryan said. "And be funny."

Tones did his best, but privately I thought he would have learned more if Ryan had given him another couple of observations about the teachers. Still, Tones seemed pleased, especially when Ryan told him he was really improving.

After about ten minutes Ryan turned to me. "You take over for a bit," he said.

"Me?"

"Yeah, you're already good at this sort of thing." Ryan smiled. "Anyway, I gotta have a crap, so I may be some time."

"Nice." I made a face, then slipped into the chair Ryan had vacated.

As Tones droned on with some interminable story about how he had been amusingly rude to his maths teacher – a story I suspected he had witnessed rather than actively participated in – my mind drifted off to Eve and whether Ryan was right about the Angle thing.

". . . so d'you think that'll work, Luke?"

I blinked, taking a second to register Tones was speaking to me.

"Sure," I said, then, feeling guilty, lied: "Ryan's right. You're doing great."

Tones grinned self-consciously. "I'm gonna ask Kirsty out, this week. Ry thinks I'm ready. I've bin chatting to her for a couple of weeks now. I can't wait any longer."

"Kirsty?" I said.

"Yeah. She's the year below us. Short. She's got curly red hair and freckles."

I frowned, unable to place her.

Tones' eyes lit up. "She's amazing."

I stared at him, wondering if it was possible that Kirsty was anywhere near as hot as Eve. I decided she couldn't be. No one was.

After the weekend I was no longer grounded. On Monday I went to the shops after school and bought a bag of wooden buttons, ready for Art Club later in the week. When I came home, Mum and Chloe were in the middle of this massive row about the fact that Chloe was still grounded for another three weeks while I was allowed to go out. They'd been arguing a lot since the party. In fact, Chloe had basically been in one, long, bad mood for weeks. She hadn't used to be like that. Not that she and Mum didn't argue. But, before, with Dad, it was different.

I set down my buttons on my bed and closed the door.

Dad used to make them laugh. When Mum and Chloe had their rows and Chloe would storm off to her room, he'd go from one to the other, coaxing them round, making them smile, until they'd calm down and come to the kitchen and . . . and somehow Dad would be there, making it all right.

I looked over at the records, still in the corner.

I could see Dad now, really clearly, peering round my bedroom door and rolling his eyes. "What is it with girls, Luke?" he'd sigh. Then he'd wink at me. "Can't live with them. Can't live without them, eh?"

I don't remember what I said back. Nothing, probably.

I sat, staring at the records, listening to Mum and Chloe shouting. They sounded like they were crying. For a second I felt like crying too. Then a door slammed and the house went quiet and I felt nothing.

Nothing at all.

At last it was Thursday. I arrived five minutes late for Art Club, hoping Eve would be there already and Ms Patel would suggest I joined her table. But Eve wasn't there. Worse – she didn't turn up later, either. After half an hour I wandered over to the two girls I'd seen her chatting to the week before.

"I wanted to ask Eve something about my collage project," I said. "D'you know if she's coming."

One of the girls half looked up at me. "She's gone to watch her boyfriend in a football match."

I walked back to my table and stared down at the stupid piles of buttons on my piece of paper.

What the hell was I doing?

I felt this tremendous urge to hurl the table over on its side. Eve was totally into Ben. I was wasting my time even thinking about her.

And then she walked in.

8

Staying late

He looks through his window
What does he see?
He sees the bright and hollow sky
He sees the stars come out tonight
He sees the city's ripped backsides
He sees the winding ocean drive
And everything was made for you and me
All of it was made for you and me . . .

'The Passenger'
Iggy Pop

Eve's face was flushed, as if she'd been running. And there was a dusting of raindrops on her hair.

Without taking off her coat she rushed over to Ms Patel. "Is it all right if I stay late?" she said. "I promise I'll clear up afterwards."

My stomach flipped over.

Ms Patel pursed her lips.

Say yes, Ms Patel. Say yes and I'll make you the best wooden-button music collage you've ever seen.

"All right, Eve," she said. "But only for half an hour. The caretaker locks up at six."

Eve pulled off her coat and raced over to the tray that I knew contained her collage. She pulled the paper out and carried it carefully to the nearest table.

I bent over my buttons. I'd wasted the last hour looking up at the door every ten seconds, but now I had a plan and I worked as if my life depended on it. I arranged the buttons in zigzagging lines across the page, then waited for Ms Patel to walk past.

A few minutes later she arrived at my table. "So how's your work going, Luke?" she said.

"Good," I said. "The wavy lines are sort of sound vibrations, but there's something missing. It needs some sort of background."

Ms Patel examined my work. "Well, I suppose you could paint a background." She looked at me doubtfully. I could tell she was remembering last week's alien-head flowers.

"I was thinking of a collage within a collage," I said. "Putting torn-up pictures of people playing music under the buttons."

Ms Patel nodded thoughtfully. "Mmmn, there's a nice dissonance in that. Well, the old newspapers we use for

69

papier-mâché are by the sink. Or you can ask Eve if she has any spare magazines."

I nodded, grinning.

At five-thirty everyone else started packing up. I looked up from the pile of newspapers I'd been examining. Ms Patel was picking up her bag. She glanced at me as she walked to the door.

"I'll just be a couple of minutes," I said.

She nodded and walked out, leaving me and Eve alone.

Alone. The space between us stretched out like an ocean. Eve was oblivious to me, her head bent over her work, her tongue peeking between her lips as she concentrated on sticking a piece of paper with glue.

My heart pounded as I walked towards her. *Look up at me. Look up.*

She looked up and smiled – a warm, genuine, friendly smile. "Hi," she said. "How's your collage going?"

"Good, thanks. I wanted to ask you. D'you have any spare magazines I could use?"

She nodded and pointed to a pile by her feet. "Those are ones I've finished with – I've taken so much out of them there's no point keeping them. You can have what you like."

I bent down and picked up the magazines.

"So what's your coursework about?" I said, looking at the paper spread out on her table. It was divided into four sections. Each section was made up of tiny scraps of paper. In one the papers were all blue, in another different shades of red. The other two were whites and greys/blacks.

"This is just the background," she said. "It's going to be a face from the Eighties. Cut-up and stuck-together bits of my mum's face from when she was a model. I'm really behind. That's why I came back to work on it tonight."

I racked my brain for something to say other than: *Is your mum as hot as you?*

"Sounds more interesting than a football match," I said.

Eve laughed. Not a high-pitched giggle like every other girl I knew – but a throaty, grown-up laugh. "You're not wrong. I got freezing cold watching."

"Who won?" I said, not liking the way our conversation seemed to be taking a turn Ben-wards.

"Ben." Eve blushed. "I mean, Ben's team. They were going out to the pub to celebrate, but I didn't feel like it."

She looked up at me. There was just the faintest hint of laughter in her eyes, as if what she was really saying was: *I wanted to come here and see you.*

I backed away, holding my magazines. I must be reading her wrong. There was no way she could blush about her boyfriend and flirt with me in the same sentence.

"Thanks for these," I said, my mouth suddenly dry.

Eve was still looking at me. "Hey, why don't we put on

71

some music?" she said. "Maybe it'll give you a bit of inspiration – you know, for your collage."

She glided across the room to Ms Patel's desk and switched on the radio. Her teeth bit lightly into her bottom lip as she twiddled the dial.

White noise, a blast of rap, something classical.

Then a dance record came on. I hadn't heard it before. A woman was singing, her voice whirling round this steady bass.

"Oh, I love this," Eve said. She twirled away from the desk into a pool of sunlight flowing in from the low sun outside the window. She swayed from side to side, her hips rippling in small circles in time with the beat.

"What is it?" I croaked, trying hard to keep my eyes on her face.

"It's a cover of 'The Passenger'. Here, come and dance."

She held out her hands towards me.

Somehow I managed to cross the room without falling over. Eve grinned at me as I arrived at the big teacher's desk. "You might want to put those down," she said.

I looked down. The pile of magazines was still in my arms. I laid them carefully on the desk, hoping Eve couldn't see my hands shaking. For a second I stood awkwardly in front of her.

What did she want me to do exactly? Normally I quite

like dancing, and I think I'm OK at it too – not brilliant, but not one of those dorks who thinks it's cool to flail around all over the place either. But right now I was lost. My legs felt like jelly. Eve was twisting and turning in the sunlight in front of me, like some kind of sexy angel. And I was trying to work out whether I should just shuffle about a bit where I was or go right up to her and . . .

She made the decision for me, by reaching out for my hand and pulling me closer, into the circle of sunlight on the floor. As I started moving in time with the music she dropped my hand. But we were still moving together, only half a metre apart, staring into each other's eyes.

I bet that sounds really hot.

In fact it was quite possibly the most terrifying experience of my life. I was nearly sick. All I could think about the whole time was when the music was going to finish and whether I could avoid collapsing before it did. The more I tried to move smoothly, the more I felt I was jerking about like a robot on speed.

At last the song was over and the DJ's rapid chatter filled the air.

We stood still for a second, staring at each other, then Eve stepped backwards, looking slightly embarrassed. "That was great, I loved the way they sampled the original 'Passenger'," she said breathlessly.

The song title connected with something in my head. "Hey," I grinned. "I think I've got the original. Was it Iggy Pop?"

Eve nodded.

"It's one of the records my dad left me."

Eve's eyes widened. "Your dad left you vintage records?"

Thank you, Dad. Thank you, Dad.

"Yeah, from the late Seventies and early Eighties. Would you like to come back to my house and hear them?"

As soon as the words were out of my mouth I knew I'd made a terrible mistake.

Eve visibly shrank away from me. "Er, no, I'm meeting Ben later." She glanced at her watch. "In fact I've gotta go now. Shoot. And I hardly got any work done either."

She bustled back to her table and cleared away her stuff. She didn't even look at me as she said goodbye.

I walked around for about half an hour. What had I done wrong? One minute she was asking me to dance with her – the next she couldn't get away from me fast enough.

I ended up outside Ryan's house. I'd only been there once before and didn't know the street number, but I recognised the iron gate, hanging off its hinges, at the end of the tiny front path.

Ryan's mum, a tall, smiley woman with the same wide mouth as Ryan, opened the door.

"Ry – aaan," she yelled up the stairs. "Friend for you."

Ryan appeared on his landing a few seconds later. He looked surprised when he saw me and not, I have to say, in a good way. He trotted down the stairs towards me, clearly annoyed.

"What is it, man?" he hissed, dragging me off into a small living room where an enormous TV was blaring into empty space.

I told him.

"I don't get it," I said. "How did I blow it?"

Ryan rolled his eyes. "You haven't blown it," he said. "Though you didn't stick to the Steps I told you to. What happened to your 'being cool' Angle? And why did you get so heavy? You were supposed to make her laugh, man, not terrify her into running away."

I groaned. It was true. Practically begging Eve to come home with me was hardly acting humorous and aloof.

"It's like I sent her into Ben's arms."

Ryan sighed. "It's always so all or nothing with you. I expect she just started feeling guilty about him. Look on the bright side. At least you know she's interested."

"She is?"

"For God's sake, man." Ryan shook his head in frustration.

75

"She asked you to *dance* with her. In the art room at school. You should have just kissed her."

"You told me not to be pushy," I snapped.

Ryan grinned. "You bottled it, didn't you? There's a time and a place, man. Situation like that, you either seize the moment, or you leave stuff unsaid. What you don't do is invite someone back to your bedroom to listen to your records. It's either gonna come out dorky or creepy. Anyway, I gotta go back upstairs."

"Oh, right," I said, bitterly. "Got some amazingly hot babe up there, have you?"

"As a matter of fact, yes." Ryan lowered his voice, so I could only just hear him over the TV. "But my mum does-n't know she's there. That's why I gotta get back."

I noticed for the first time that Ryan's shirt was untucked and the back of his hair was all rumpled up.

"Who is it?" I said, trying not to sound envious.

"Like I'm gonna tell *you*." Ryan winked at me. "She's totally Premiership, though."

He edged towards the door.

Half-term started tomorrow, which meant it would be two weeks until I saw Eve again at Art Club. I remembered what Ben had said in the burger bar and realised, with a sickening lurch, that would be the week of her sixteenth birthday.

I wanted to ask Ryan what he thought I should do next, but knowing he had some girl upstairs waiting for him made it just too humiliating. So we walked out to the front door in silence.

"I'll come round later," Ryan said. "We can talk about Step Five then. I think it could help."

"Whatever," I grunted – knowing, and not caring, that I sounded ungrateful.

As I walked home I saw Tones going in the opposite direction, his arm round a short, plump, red-haired girl whose face was as covered with freckles as his was with spots.

Kirsty.

I didn't want to cramp his style, so I just gave him a friendly wink as we passed each other. He looked like he might explode with pride.

Oh well. At least the Six Steps had worked for someone. Seeing Tones looking so happy cheered me up a bit. And Ryan was right. Eve *had* wanted to dance with me. My mind filled with how amazingly horny she'd looked, pulling me towards her in that patch of sunlight.

As soon as I got home I went up to my room, played my dad's single of 'The Passenger' and let myself think about her, over and over again.

9

Listening

Peeling the skin back from my eyes – I felt surprise
That the time on the clock was the time – I usually retired
To the place where I cleared my head of you
But, just for today, I think I'll lie here and dream of you

'Uncertain Smile'
The The

It was Friday, about eight o'clock. Chloe had just snuck in and she and Mum were having yet another row – they were averaging about three a day at the moment. I could hear them from my room, even over the music I was playing.

"How dare you speak to me like that?" Mum yelled.

"Because you're a total bitch," Chloe yelled back. "Nobody gets grounded for a month. Nobody. It's totally unfair."

I turned the volume up on Dad's old record player as high as it would go.

I'd played all his records now. Some of them weren't bad, though I still didn't understand why he'd given them to me. I'd decided it wasn't worth feeling hurt about it. After all, not having anything in common with your dad's not such a big deal.

The music finished and the needle hissed as it flopped off the turntable. I lifted it back onto its arm. This old technology was rubbish. Imagine having to get up and down every time you wanted to put on a new track? The sound quality was the worst thing, though. It had taken me ages to get used to all the crackle and static that existed as permanent background noise under the music.

Everything was quiet downstairs. And I was starving. Hoping Chloe had flounced off to her room, I padded down to the kitchen. Mum and Uncle Matt were sitting at the kitchen table. I could hear Mum sniffing as I reached the door. Matt was patting her on the back.

"D'you want me to speak to her?"

Mum shook her head. "Maybe Luke could."

"Me?" I said from the door.

They both looked up. Matt reddened a little and whipped his hand off Mum's back. Mum smiled weakly at me.

"I just thought you might be able to get through to her," she said, her voice crumpling to a whisper. "She hates me."

79

"She doesn't hate you, Mum," I said, striding to the fridge. "She's just mad at you for grounding her for a whole month."

"That doesn't excuse her language and the terrible way she treats your mother." Matt bristled.

Butt out. Nobody asked you.

I turned my back and began rummaging in the fridge.

"I was trying to talk to her about Dad's ashes," Mum said. "I picked them up today."

I took out a carton of milk and turned round. My eyes fell on a small wooden box on the table between Mum and Matt.

"Is that . . . them?" I asked.

How freak-show was that? Dad's body sitting here on our kitchen table. I stared at the box. I couldn't connect it with Dad at all. It was just a box.

"I was asking Chloe where she thought we should scatter them," Mum sniffed. "And . . . and she turned on me and demanded to know why she should even discuss it, if I wasn't going to let her out of the house. As if I'd stop her being part of . . . oh . . ." Mum dissolved into tears. She put her face in her hands.

Shit. I wanted to say something to make her feel better. But I didn't know what. And, anyway, Matt was already talking.

"It's the attitude that gets me," he said, patting her arm. "When I was growing up, kids had a bit of respect for their parents." He gave me a hard stare.

I glared back.

"I pointed out to your sister," Matt went on, not taking his eyes off me, "that I was your dad's best friend. And that I'm here because I want to help."

I turned back to the fridge, severely rattled. I was fed up with Matt coming round every five minutes, getting in the middle of our family business.

". . . well, Luke? What do you think?"

I realised Mum had been talking to me again, presumably about the stupid ashes. I put back the pint of milk and straightened up.

"Honestly, Mum?" I said, walking to the door. "I think we should put Dad's ashes on the mantelpiece in the living room." I turned as I reached the door and stared straight at Matt. "After all, this is Dad's house."

Ryan and Numbers arrived about half an hour later.

"I'm not stopping," Numbers grinned. "Just wanted to let you know I've had twenty-five, hands-on snogs since I last saw you."

"How interesting," I said. "How many of them were with humans?"

Undaunted, Numbers grinned smugly. Then he turned and set off down the street.

Ryan shook his head. "Sometimes I wish I'd never met Numbers. He does my head in. Anyway, I thought we should talk."

"Right," I said. "Let's go out. It's a war zone in here."

"OK, I just need to use your bathroom then," Ryan said, quickly.

"Don't you ever go at home?" I said.

But Ryan had already darted past me and was vanishing up the stairs. A few minutes later he came back down and we wandered along to the high street. There's this open, concrete space by the Town Hall where kids hang out. Older ones at night. Younger ones early evening. I used to skateboard here a long time ago.

"Step Five," Ryan said, "is Attention. The Steps so far have worked, haven't they? I mean you're making more effort with how you look – Step One. You got her to notice you back in the art room, even though you weren't trying exactly – Step Two. You've found an Angle, not being all pushy with her, which was Step Three . . ." he paused, "even if you're not solid on it. And you know you can make her laugh – Step Four. Even though you haven't done it yet." He threw me a frustrated glance. "Anyway, so long as you've been completely clear that friendship's not an option, then Step Five's the killer. Attention."

"What d'you mean?" I said. "Flowers? Compliments? What?"

Ryan grinned. "That stuff's good. Chicks lap it up, in fact. But the most important thing you gotta learn to do is Listening."

I kicked at the edge of the pavement. Listening didn't sound so hard. "I can do that," I said. "No problem."

"Actually, you're crap at listening."

I frowned at him. "No, I'm not."

"How many times in the last week have you totally tuned out while people were talking to you? So that they've gone all: 'Luke, Luke, are you listening to me?'. Think about it."

I stared down at the pavement. Now Ryan put it like that, I realised he was right. It had happened with Mum earlier; with Tones the other day. And it had happened with Eve in the art room too.

"I reckon you'd have got a lot further with Eve if you'd bothered to really concentrate on her. And I don't mean on how hot she is."

"But how . . .?" I stopped. *How on earth am I supposed to listen to what she says, when my head's so full of the way she looks?*

"I know it's hard." Ryan was looking at me shrewdly. "You gotta distract yourself – forget about how horned-up you are and listen to what she's saying, like it's . . . like she's about to tell you something you really want to know . . . like a football score or something."

I screwed up my face. "Even if she's talking rubbish?"

"*Especially* then. What seems like rubbish to you could be really important to her. You can't ever tell. Girls don't always say what they mean. In fact, they often don't. So you have to listen really hard – not just to what she's saying, but the way she's talking and how she's looking at you. Then you'll know when to make your move."

It sounded totally impossible. I shook my head.

"Don't worry." Ryan grinned. "After a while you'll find you can focus on what she's saying, work out what she really means *and* still have room in your head to think about what you'd like to do with her – all at the same time."

I stared at him. It was dark where we were standing and the open space in front of the Town Hall was totally empty.

"How do you know all this stuff, Ry?" I said.

He shrugged. "Dunno, really. I guess the main thing was . . . this girl I met. It was after some gig I went to a while back, with a couple of my older sisters. I . . . I sort of ended up with one of their friends. We hooked up for a bit. She taught me a lot . . ."

I raised my eyebrows.

Ryan grinned again. "Yeah, that. But also what works when you're talking to someone, and how most girls think boys their age are really immature, so acting more grown-up's like this big turn-on. Then, after that, I just started watching and learning. And practising . . ." He tailed off.

"So who you practising on now?"

Ryan winked at me. "You know I can't say." He checked the time on his mobile. "She's a babe, though. In fact, I gotta go. I'm meeting her later."

He slouched off up the road. I watched him go, an uneasy feeling in the pit of my stomach. I liked Ryan. But he wasn't like any other guy I'd ever met. There was all the stuff he knew about girls. And then this mystery babe business. I mean, it wasn't like Ryan not to boast about the girls he'd been with. And on top of all that – the way he went out of his way to help me. I mean, what was he getting out of it? It just didn't add up.

Not particularly wanting to go home, I strolled over to the glassed screens in front of the Town Hall and looked at the advertisements for local events. Nothing very interesting. Posters for band gigs, notices about local theatre group plays and postcard ads for au pairs and cleaners.

My mind drifted to Eve. Tomorrow was Friday. The last day before half-term. My last opportunity to speak to Eve for ten days. Possibly my last opportunity before her birthday.

An exhibition poster showing a woman with blonde hair caught my eye. I stared at it. And then it came to me. A wholly brilliant idea.

I smiled.

Suddenly, I knew exactly what to do.

I watched out for Eve all Friday morning. No sign. I was starting to think she wasn't even at school today, when I saw her in the cafeteria.

Ben had his hands all over her in the lunch queue.

I walked off in disgust.

I rushed outside when the bell rang at the end of the day. People streamed past me. My heart thumped. It was too noisy. Too busy. I was going to miss her completely.

And then I saw her, chatting to her two Art Club friends. I hadn't envisaged doing what I was about to do with an audience, but the three of them were all moving towards the school gates. If I left it any longer I'd be following them down the road like a stalker.

I tried to saunter ever so casually in Eve's direction,

hoping she'd see me and acknowledge me in some way. She didn't. I had to walk up to the whole group before she even noticed me.

"Hi," I said.

They all turned round. Eve gave a half-hearted sort of smile; the other two glared at me.

Great.

Well, I was here now. I might as well go ahead with it.

"Thought you might like to know," I said, trying to control the shake in my voice, "there's an exhibition of Eighties' stuff on at Finlays Gallery near the Town Hall. I know you're interested in all that."

See Ryan? I was listening.

Eve said nothing. Sweat trickled down the back of my neck.

"It closes on Monday," I lied, ultra-casually. "Just thought it might be useful for your coursework."

One of the other girls sniffed impatiently, but my eyes were fixed on Eve's. What she did now determined everything.

"What time does it close?" she said slowly.

"Midday Monday," I said. "I'm going there Monday morning."

Please be there.

"Right, thanks," Eve said.

I stared at her. What had Ryan said? *It's not just what they say, it's the way they talk and how they look at you.*

It was no good. I couldn't read the expression in Eve's eyes at all. Her friends were starting to shuffle about, staring at me.

I turned on my heel and walked off, my hands coolly in my pockets, my heart pumping like a train.

10

The gallery

Darling, you gotta let me know
Should I stay or should I go?
If you say that you are mine
I'll be here till the end of time.
So you got to let me know
Should I stay or should I go?

'Should I Stay Or Should I Go'
The Clash

I knew the gallery opened at ten on Monday morning.

I was ready at nine.

It had been a long, boring weekend. I'd played foot
with some of my old mates on Saturday, then Rya
come round on Sunday. Mum asked him if he w
stay for lunch, and for once, we had a meal that
with Chloe storming off to her room.

It was like before Dad died. Everyone

getting on. And then Ryan had to leave and, within seconds, Mum and Chloe were fighting again – this time over the washing-up.

It was like they were so strung out with each other that one word from either of them was enough to set the other one off.

I was sick of it.

I spent the rest of the weekend shut up in my room. Eve was always there, in my head. But it wasn't enough anymore.

I wanted her. I wanted the real thing.

I didn't let myself think about the possibility that she might not show up at the gallery.

I'd never taken so much trouble getting ready to go out before. First off, I showered and tried a bit of Chloe's wax in my hair. Course, I used way too much and my hair went like cardboard. So I had to shower all over again. Then I spent fifteen minutes trying to decide what to wear. I had no idea what Eve would think looked good. I badly wanted to ask Chloe, but a) she would have totally sussed me if I had and b) she hadn't yet emerged from her own bedroom.

In the end I settled on a blue T-shirt, a thick, black jumper and jeans. I put it all on, then – remembering something Ryan had said weeks ago – took off the T-shirt and ironed it, just in case.

When Mum walked into the kitchen and saw me bent over the ironing board she blinked with surprise.

"Oh, Luke." She sat down at the kitchen table with a sigh. "Why is it you're coping so well and Chloe's gone to pieces?"

I hate it when she asks me questions like that. I mean, there aren't any answers, are there?

I shrugged and unplugged the iron.

Once I was ready, I mooched round the house for about half an hour. It was only going to take about fifteen minutes to get down to the gallery.

At last I decided it was time to go. I yelled goodbye to Mum, but before I was out the front door, she appeared in the hall.

"Before you go out, sweetheart," she said, "there's something I'd like you to do."

Crap.

"Mum, I'm busy. I'm meeting someone."

She twisted her hands together. "It won't take long. It's just . . ."

"What?"

"It's Chloe. I've been banging on her door and she's not answering. And she's locked it *again*. Even though I've told her not to a hundred times."

Mum's eyes were filling with tears. I put my arms round

her and hugged her, silently cursing Chloe for being such a pain.

"She's probably still asleep, Mum. Look, I've really got to—"

"Will you get up on the porch and look through her window?" Mum asked.

I stared at her. "*What . . .?*"

"It's just occurred to me," Mum sniffed, "she could be getting out of the house without me knowing, then leaving her door locked from the inside, so that I'll think she's still in there."

"And you want me to get on the roof and spy through her window?" I said. "Jesus, Mum, that's going a bit far, isn't it?"

"Luke, she's totally out of control. I wish to God I hadn't grounded her for as long as I did. I should have realised that that party of hers was just a reaction to Dad dying. Maybe if I'd gone a bit easier on her, she wouldn't have gone off the rails like this."

"I don't think—"

"Please, Luke. You know I'll get all dizzy if I go up there myself. I could ask Matt, but if—"

"No, I'll do it," I said.

Anything to keep Uncle pigging Matt out of our business.

I checked my watch. Twenty to ten. It would only take a couple of minutes to get onto the porch roof. Still plenty of time to make it down to the gallery by ten.

I clambered onto the porch wall, then hooked my arm over the roof. I heard a rip as the jagged edge of a tile caught in my sleeve and tore up a line of wool. *Excellent.* I hauled myself onto the roof, thinking there was no way Chloe would ever consider doing this. She goes nuts if she chips a nail.

"Be careful, sweetheart," Mum called up from the front garden.

The roof sloped upwards slightly, and I had to lean into it so as not to slip down. I took two tentative steps across to Chloe's window. It was open just a finger's width at the bottom. I grabbed the ledge with my hands and peered into her room, convinced she would still be asleep. But the bed was empty. It wasn't a large room and I could see every corner from where I was standing. Chloe wasn't there.

"Well?" Mum called.

I thought quickly. If I told her the truth, Mum would totally lose it. She'd almost certainly call the police – after all, Chloe could have been gone all night. I looked round the room again. No, I was sure she'd at least slept in the bed. The duvet was all ruckled up and a pair of pyjamas lay strewn across the floor between the bed and the

93

wardrobe. Anyway, Chloe could look after herself. But Mum wasn't likely to see it that way, which meant there would be no chance of me getting away to the gallery. Plus, once Chloe reappeared, Mum would ground her again. Which would mean no end to all the rows that were doing my head in.

It was an easy decision to make.

"She's asleep, Mum," I shouted, "with her headphones on. That's why she can't hear you knocking."

As I clambered off the roof I eased my conscience with the thought that when Chloe finally came home, I would tell her how I'd covered for her – and demand that she stopped sneaking out.

Mum hugged me. "Thanks, sweetheart," she said. "I don't know what I'd do without you."

Feeling guilty, I jogged off down the road.

It was five past ten when I arrived at the gallery. There was no sign of Eve outside, so I went in and had a quick look round. It was a small building with just three rooms full of pictures and posters and a bored-looking woman at the front desk. There was no one else there. I sat outside on the steps for a while, staring up at the advertisement for the exhibition. *Faces of the Eighties.*

By eleven o'clock the exhibition had had fewer than five

visitors and there was still no sign of Eve. I was hungry and freezing and trying not to listen to the voice in my head which kept telling me she wasn't coming. I decided that as long as I was here, I might as well go inside and look at the posters.

The woman at the front desk was reading a magazine. She didn't look up as I went through to the first room. I wandered from picture to picture, looking at the faces with their weird hair and old-fashioned clothes. I grinned as I walked past a picture of a man naked to the waist, holding a baby. A pair of old ladies – the only other people in the building at the moment – had been standing in front of it for several minutes, tutting about how disgusting it was that he wasn't wearing a shirt.

I stopped in front of a poster of a mini-skirted woman with straggly blonde hair. The caption underneath said: *Deborah Harry, lead singer with the band, Blondie.* I vaguely remembered one of Dad's records was by Blondie. The woman was hot. Massively.

I stared at her, wondering if my dad had ever fancied her.

"You can put your tongue away," said a soft, raspy voice in my ear. "She's about a hundred now."

I spun round. Eve was standing behind me, her lips curled in a mocking smile.

My stomach did several somersaults in quick succession. I could feel my face reddening. Eve's smile broadened with delight at my embarrassment.

"Come on, there's something I want to show you," she said.

She grabbed my arm and dragged me into the next room. I was still in a state of total confusion when she stopped at a picture halfway down the wall. It showed the face of another blonde woman, this time on the cover of a magazine – I didn't notice the title. I stared at the woman. Her pale blue eyes looked coyly up out of the picture through thick, black lashes.

I knew immediately who she was.

"She's beautiful," I said.

"That's my mum," Eve said, proudly. "When she was twenty-one. I wish I looked like her."

I glanced at her. "You do," I said.

Eve flushed slightly, but didn't say anything. We walked together round the whole exhibition. Neither of us mentioned the fact that we both knew it wasn't closing at midday. Eve knew loads about some of the pictures – she'd already been round last week with her mum. It crossed my mind to ask Eve why she was here again, but she soon supplied the answer herself.

She loved the exhibition.

We walked round slowly, Eve chattering away, her eyes shining. Most of what she said about the pictures wasn't very interesting, to be honest. But I tried hard to listen. Or, at least, to look as if I was listening. It was difficult not to be distracted by her face, especially when her lips stretched into that slow, sexy smile of hers.

At last we came to the final picture. And then there was nothing else to do except leave. We strolled out to the front desk.

There was an awkward silence.

"I've got to meet my mum," Eve said. "I was supposed to be shopping with her all morning. I had to make an excuse to come here."

She looked at me. I tried to work out whether there was some kind of hidden message in what she was saying.

"Ben's away all half-term on some football trip," she said.

Oh, good, let's talk about Ben again.

"Right," I said, determined to turn the subject away from her stupid boyfriend. "Chloe's grounded all half-term. It's her third week, she's going mental with it. I think she's even sneaking out of the house."

But Eve didn't seem to want to talk about Chloe any more than I wanted to talk about Ben.

We walked outside onto the pavement. We were on a side road off the high street. Where the two roads met, about thirty metres away, traffic was zooming past. It filled our silence with a noisy hum.

"Well I guess I'd better get off and meet my mum," Eve said, again. She was staring at me, as if waiting for something. I started to panic. Jesus, what was she expecting me to do now?

Ask for her phone number?

Surely not, after she just mentioned Ben.

Ask her if she wants to go for a coffee?

No, you idiot, she's already said she's got to meet her mum.

What about seeing her later?

Suppose she flips out again and runs off? No. Get a grip. Be cool.

"This was fun," I said, playing for time. "Interesting."

She smiled. "Yeah, Ben would have hated it."

My face fell. *Great. Back to Ben again.*

"I mean I'm glad I was here with you." Eve moved the tiniest bit closer to me. She kept her eyes fixed on mine, then she tilted her head back slightly.

A thrill of anticipation tingled down my spine. I suddenly knew exactly what she was waiting for me to do.

I moved closer to her. Her pale eyes were all I could see. The art gallery, the traffic sounds from the high street, the people passing by . . . They all fell away.

I moved even closer.

When she spoke I could feel her breath on my mouth.

"I shouldn't do this," she whispered.

Our lips were so close they were almost touching.

"I know," I murmured.

I closed my eyes and the whole world exploded in my head.

I pulled away, shivering.

Eve was still standing there, her eyes shut.

She drew in a tiny breath, like a soft whispery gasp.

It was about the sexiest thing I'd ever heard in my life.

She opened her eyes and drew back. A look of confusion crossed her face.

I was desperate to kiss her again. But I wasn't going to have her run out on me a second time, like she had in the art room.

"See you then," I said.

Before she could reply I'd turned and walked away, praying my legs would hold me up until I got round the corner and out of sight.

11

Lunch party

I'll be the ticket if you're my collector
I've got the fare if you're my inspector
I'll be the luggage, if you'll be the porter
I'll be the parcel if you'll be my sorter

'Love Song'
The Damned

I walked halfway up the high street in a blissful, sexed-up daze. All I wanted to do was relive that kiss. How Eve had looked at me. How her mouth had felt. How she'd tasted.

All that stuff about Ben – how she'd gone on about him being away. None of that mattered. She'd kissed me. She'd *wanted* to kiss me.

I stopped, a sudden realisation hitting me like a bucket of cold water. How could I have been so stupid? Telling me Ben was away this week was obviously Eve's way of saying I could see her again before he got back. And I'd walked away without even asking for her phone number. I groaned out loud. It was all Ryan's fault with his stupid Steps. "Get an Angle." "Be aloof."

Be aloof, my arse.

Why the hell hadn't I asked if I could call her? I hadn't even had her stupid friends watching me this time, and I'd still managed to blow it. Of course, Chloe probably had Eve's number, but unless I could sneak a look at her mobile (which Chloe practically slept with) there was no way I would find it. And even then . . . *oh crap* . . . Eve would think I was such an idiot . . . and Ben would get back and my chance would be over.

It's strange. A week ago, just imagining an actual kiss would have kept me going for days. But now, with my brain reeling from my own stupidity, it felt like having one sip of drink when you're dying of thirst. Amazing. But not enough. Nowhere near enough.

Chloe was curled up on the living-room sofa when I got home. She looked tired – there were dark rings under her eyes and her face was pale. I remembered how she hadn't been in her room earlier and felt a twinge of curiosity about where she had been. And then I had an idea.

"Must be boring not being allowed out," I said, flinging myself down in Dad's armchair.

She looked at me sulkily. "Pig off," she said.

God, why did she have to be such a moody cow? I pushed myself up, crossed the room and closed the door in case Mum was anywhere nearby. Then I turned on Chloe. "If I were you I'd start being a bit nicer to me. You owe me big time."

Chloe glanced up at me, irritatingly uninterested. "What are you talking about?"

I told her.

"I can't believe Mum set you to spy on me like that," Chloe said.

"Never mind that. Where the hell were you?"

Chloe shrugged. "Out. Just seeing some friends."

"Well, you gotta stop. Next time she'll get Matt to go up there and have a look." I paused. "Why don't you ask your friends to come round here?"

Chloe raised her eyebrows. "Anyone in particular?"

"No," I said, quickly. What did she mean? Did she know about Eve? No, how could she? I must be imagining it. "I just thought it might be a good idea."

Chloe shrugged again. "Whatever. Anyway, thanks for not grassing me up."

Chloe said nothing for the rest of the day, but the following morning she was downstairs before ten o'clock, a list in her hand.

She shoved the list across the kitchen table to Mum. "I've invited some friends round for lunch," she snapped. "And we need some food for it, which *you'll* have to get because *I'm* not allowed out."

Mum's face clenched up and went red. "How dare you assume you can just—?"

"It's OK, Mum." I jumped up and grabbed the list. "I'll get the food."

They both looked at me, astonished. I shrugged. "I was going out anyway," I lied.

Mum was still pretty annoyed with Chloe for having invited her friends round without checking first. And she spent a good ten minutes insisting that Chloe didn't need both Hawaiian *and* pepperoni pizzas, but eventually she gave me some money and I escaped into the fresh air. A warm breeze drifted across my face. It felt like the first day of spring.

I did the shopping as quickly as I could, wondering the whole time how I could find out if Chloe had invited Eve.

"Luke – you got completely the wrong type of pizza," Chloe moaned from the kitchen. "And the salad's past its sell-by date."

It was twelve-thirty and, typically, Chloe had only just arrived downstairs to start sorting out her lunch stuff.

Mum winked at me. "I'm sure Luke did his best," she called out. We were in the living room. I still hadn't managed to discover if Eve was coming, and I was trying to keep my mind off the subject by watching TV. I'd decided that if she did turn up, my best bet was to be cool and relaxed, but to drop some hint about where I'd be hanging out tomorrow.

The doorbell went. I got up. "I'll get it."

Two of Chloe's classmates stood on the steps. They were deep in conversation and barely muttered a "hello" as they passed. Five minutes later another friend turned up and ten minutes after that, a fourth.

That had to be it. Chloe'd only bought four pizzas, after all. Then the door sounded again. Mum was in the hall. I heard her open the door. "Hello, Eve," she said. "Don't you look nice."

I went out into the hall as Mum stepped back to let Eve in.

My breath caught in my throat as I looked at her.

Yesterday, I hadn't noticed what Eve was wearing. Just a long, shapeless jacket, zipped up to the neck, I think. There couldn't have been a greater contrast with what she had on now.

High-heeled, knee-length boots, a short skirt and a very clingy blue jumper. Her hair was all sleek and shiny and tied back in a ponytail which snaked round onto her shoulders. She caught my eye and smiled.

"Hi, Luke," she said. She sashayed past me down the hall and into the kitchen. I turned and watched her, my mouth open.

"For goodness' sake, Luke," Mum hissed, prodding me in the ribs as she passed.

I staggered back into the living room. All thoughts of playing it cool vanished. I didn't care if I ended up looking a total prat. I had to get Eve on her own again. Today. I couldn't see anything beyond that.

I sat down and forced myself to work out what I should do. Eve wouldn't be here for long. An hour maybe, if I was lucky. She'd arrived later than everyone else. For all I knew she was about to dash off to meet her mum again.

But I could hardly go up to her surrounded by Chloe and all their friends. I strode back into the hall, to where Chloe's army of handbags lay in a messy cluster at the bottom of the stairs. I rummaged through them, trying to find Chloe's phone.

I knew that if Chloe caught me I would never hear the end of it.

I didn't care.

No sign of the mobile. Course not. Chloe always carried it with her. It must be in the kitchen. Praying that Chloe wasn't wearing anything with pockets, I marched straight in there. I could feel six pairs of eyes follow me across the room to the counter where Chloe had been preparing the pizzas and salad.

"What do you want?" Chloe said.

I looked round, determined not to look directly at Eve.

"I'm hungry," I said.

Chloe nodded and turned away. I could feel Eve at the other end of the table. I knew she was looking at me. With a massive effort I turned back to the counter and looked up and down. *Yes*. Chloe's phone was sitting next to the plate of cooked pizza slices. In one swift move I grabbed the phone, laid a slice of pizza on top of it, and left.

I raced up to my room, already clicking through Chloe's address book. *E. Eve*. There. I reached for my own phone and tapped in the number. I stood there, my thumb hovering over the buttons. What the hell was I going to say?

There was no time to make it look clever or mature or any of the things Ryan was always banging on about. I took a deep breath.

i hv 2 c u. Smll pnd. Waterlow Park. Luke.

Without even reading it over I pressed "send". Recklessness thrilled through me – quickly followed by a swamping feeling of dread.

I raced downstairs, then darted into the kitchen to put

106

Chloe's phone back. I kept my head down the whole time, but I could see Eve was turned away from the others, bending over her phone.

I walked straight out and went to the park. I headed for the small pond. It must have rained in the night – the grass was soggy under my tramping feet. But the air was warm – like it had been earlier – and the sun beat down on my face as I walked along the pond's squelchy banks.

If she came, it meant she was interested.

If she came it meant she wanted me to ask her out.

I stopped.

If she came, maybe it just meant she was going to tell me to stop pestering her.

I turned round and saw her, picking her way across the muddy grass towards me. She looked cross. Irritated. I gritted my teeth. OK, if I had to hear that she didn't want me, better to hear it now. Get it over with.

She stopped about two metres away from me and scowled.

"This mud's ruining my boots," she said. "I only got them yesterday."

And then she smiled, this warm, deep, gorgeously sexy smile. "D'you mind if we get off the grass?"

12

Lessons in love

Hand in glove
The sun shines out of our behinds
No, it's not like any other love
This one is different – because it's us.

'Hand In Glove'
The Smiths

We walked along the gravel path, holding hands. The part of the park I'd chosen to meet Eve in was the most secluded bit, and I had no intention of moving away from it, even if that meant we wandered in circles for hours.

Eve talked about her art project again. I tried to listen to her, like Ryan had said I should. I really did. But my mind was in about three places at once. And none of them had anything to do with collage materials. She was just so unbelievably sexy. And I wasn't the only one who thought so. I noticed several guys among the few people we passed checking her out and then throwing me envious glances.

At last we sat down on a bench and I leaned into her.

After a couple of minutes' snogging she pushed me gently away.

"What is it?" I said.

Eve bit her lip. The skin round her mouth was red. She touched it gingerly. "You're a bit rough," she said. "It feels like you're vacuuming the inside of my mouth."

I could feel my whole body shrink right down inside my clothes. "Oh," I said, now painfully aware of my neck and face burning red. "Sorry."

I looked down at the grass.

"It's OK," Eve said. "Just relax."

We started again. This time I tried to focus more on what she was doing. To match what I did with what she did.

"Mmmn," Eve said when we stopped. "That was better."

My confidence lifted. I stared at her very seriously. "You know I still need a lot of practice."

She laughed.

The sound trickled through me like honey, soothing away my remaining anxieties.

This was it. I'd done it. Steps One to Five. Sorted.

As I leaned back in for another kiss, I wondered vaguely what Step Six was. Whatever it was, I obviously didn't need it.

The sexiest, most beautiful, most amazing girl I had ever met wanted to snog me.

Me.

I was blessed. I was triumphant. I was the king of the world.

Eventually Eve said it was too cold to sit still any longer and we walked back up to the main part of the park.

As we passed the busy children's playground, Eve dropped my hand. "We've got to be careful," she said. "You know, in case Ben finds out."

Ben. I'd forgotten about his existence. I wanted her to forget it too. "I thought he was away."

"He is," Eve said. "But what if someone sees us and tells him?"

I shrugged. "Well, why don't you just tell him you're going out with me now?"

I hadn't meant to ask her quite like that. My heart thudded as I waited for her to reply.

Eve wrinkled her nose. "It's not that simple," she said.

What the hell did *that* mean?

We parted at the park gates. Eve wouldn't let me kiss her goodbye in case anyone saw us. But she did say she would meet me tomorrow morning in the same place.

*

110

And she did. Every day that week. The spring weather got warmer and drier. We met each morning and spent the whole day in the park, kissing and talking and laughing about stupid stuff to do with school and people we knew. It was bliss. Well, it was eighty per cent bliss. Ten per cent of it was humiliation – as in more criticisms of my snogging technique, though that eased up as the week went on. And ten per cent of it was sheer panic, mostly brought on by Eve's only annoying habit – a tendency to ask difficult questions.

Take this. Our second date – third, I suppose, if you count the gallery.

We were lying out on the grass (now dry, soft and springy) beside the small pond. Eve was curled up in my arms and I was just chilling out, loving the way her hair smelled all lemony and sneaking the occasional peek at the lacy edge of the bra under her top.

Out of nowhere, she sat up and stretched her arms.

"So how many girls have you been out with?" she said, casually.

I shrugged. "Dunno. A few."

"What, you can't remember?" Eve looked scandalised.

I frowned. What the hell was the right thing to say now?

"I guess it depends what you mean by 'going out'," I said. "But not many, and no one like you."

There. That should satisfy her, shouldn't it?

In your dreams, mate.

"How d'you mean 'no one like me'?" she said.

"Well, no one who looks like you, for a start."

"So how did they look?"

"Well, they looked OK, but not . . ."

"So they were pretty then?"

"Yeah, I guess . . ."

"So you've been out with lots of very pretty girls?"

"No."

"But you said . . ."

And on it went.

I couldn't understand it. Why did she need to ask all these questions? The last thing I wanted to know was how many boys she'd been out with. I had a hard enough time coping with the idea of Ben.

I liked it better when we found out practical stuff about each other, like the music we were into and our home lives. I soon discovered that Eve's parents were divorced. She lived with her mum and only saw her dad, who ran a hotel in Spain, occasionally. She asked me about my family a few times, telling me how she knew what it was like when your dad wasn't around. I didn't say much back – I mean, what was there to say? Eve also told me how everyone in their class reckoned Chloe had got this mysterious new boyfriend.

"We all think he's someone older. Maybe even a teacher. But she won't say a word."

I told Eve how Chloe had been sneaking out of her bedroom window at night, locking her door from the inside. She listened, her beautiful eyes widening into circles.

"One of these days she's going to get *sooo* busted."

I was more worried by the idea of this older boyfriend. I mean, like I said before, Chloe can look after herself. But still, I hoped she was OK. I knew Chloe would refuse to discuss it with me. I considered saying something to Mum – but only for a second or two. Chloe would never forgive me. And I couldn't imagine what the atmosphere in the house would be like if she was angry with both of us.

It was the Thursday of half-term. We were lying side by side on Eve's living-room sofa. Her mum was out and not due back until the evening.

"Maybe the boyfriend's like a father figure for Chloe," Eve said.

I ran my hand down the side of her body, into the dip of her waist, then out, over the curve of her hip. "Mmmn?" I said.

Eve wriggled backwards and sat up. She hooked back her hair and pressed her lips together in a determined line.

My heart sank. I knew that expression now. It meant she was going to ask me another impossible question.

"Chloe's boyfriend. You know, I reckon she acts all tough but underneath she's really unhappy, 'cause of your dad dying. So, maybe she's gone for someone older because he reminds her of . . . of your dad. What d'you think?"

"Eew." I made a face.

"Not *literally* like your dad." Eve rolled her eyes. "But you said they were really close. Maybe she misses him so much that she wants to be with someone more mature, more adult."

"Yeah, well," I said, seeing an opportunity to close down the conversation, "there's no point wondering, is there? I mean we don't even know if Chloe's actually got a boyfriend."

I reached out and tugged gently on Eve's hair, hoping she would lie back down next to me. But Eve caught my hand and held it.

"Do you miss your dad?" she said.

I stared at her. Even though Eve had tried to get me to talk about him several times, I hadn't really thought about Dad for weeks. To be honest, him dying still didn't feel real. It was as if he wasn't really dead, but had just gone off on some long business trip. He used to do that a lot before he got ill. Sometimes he'd be away for a month and we'd get used to him not being around. And then, suddenly, he'd be back.

I shrugged. "I wasn't really close to him."

"But still," Eve persisted, "you must feel sad that he's gone?"

How could I explain it to her? I didn't understand it myself.

"He didn't really know me," I said, staring down at the sofa. "And I didn't know him. You know all he left me was those old records I told you about." I stopped. An unexpected lump had risen in my throat.

"Maybe he thought you'd like them," Eve said, gently. "I mean, they were from when he was young."

I shook my head, not trusting myself to speak.

Eve slid down next to me on the sofa and wrapped her arms round my neck. She stared into my eyes. "Maybe they were his way of telling you he loved you."

There was something so tender about the way she was looking at me that my eyes filled with tears. I blinked them back, embarrassed.

Eve leaned forwards and kissed me on the lips. I kissed her back like she'd showed me. It was perfect. She was perfect.

And then her mobile rang.

115

Eve reached out to the table beside the sofa and groped for the phone. I didn't stop kissing her until she'd brought it right up to her mouth.

"Hi," she said, her eyes still locked onto mine.

It was as if she'd been burned. She jumped away from me and off the sofa.

"Yeah. Right. OK . . . OK," she said into the phone.

She clutched at her hair, shaking her head at me as I started to get off the sofa and walk towards her.

"No. I'm fine. Nothing's wrong."

I put my hand out to her shoulder, but she shook it off. *Jesus*. Her hands were shaking.

"OK. Yeah, babe. Me too. See you then."

I froze.

"Bye . . . yeah . . . bye."

Eve clicked the phone off and turned to me. Her pale eyes were wide with alarm – and something else . . . excitement? "That was Ben," she said. "He's coming back and he wants to see me tomorrow night."

"Well, tell him no."

"I can't," Eve said. She turned away and walked across the room.

"You mean you won't," I snapped. Anger tightened my throat. "He's a jerk. He doesn't care about you."

"You don't know him," Eve said.

116

"I've heard him talking about you, saying how he's going to 'do you' on your sixteenth birthday. And how grateful you're going to be."

Eve's eyes narrowed and her normally creamy skin flushed red.

"You're lying," she shouted. "You're just saying that 'cause you're jealous." She burst into tears.

I stood there, uncomfortably, my rage evaporating as she sobbed. I didn't know what else to do, so I walked over and put my arms round her. "I'm sorry," I said.

I held Eve until she stopped crying and drew back from me. It was amazing. Even with red eyes and smears of black make-up on her cheek, she was more beautiful than any other girl in the world.

I kissed her nose.

"Why can't I see you both?" Eve sniffed.

I stared at her. My stomach twisted into a knot. I hated the idea of sharing her with anyone. But I couldn't bear the thought of losing her either.

Eve ran her finger down my cheek.

"I don't want to stop seeing you," she whispered.

I could feel myself being pulled into her eyes. Every part of me ached for her.

"OK," I whispered back.

Nothing else mattered. Only being with Eve.

13

Busted

We've come to scream – in the happy house
We're in a dream – in the happy house
We're all quite sane.

'Happy House'
Siouxsie and the Banshees

After four days of spring weather, the temperature dropped to
almost freezing on Thursday night. Then on Friday it rained.
Eve and I met as usual in the park, but it was grey and wet
and miserable and Eve kept complaining she was cold.

We wandered out of the park and up towards the high
street. I'd been trying for hours to think of somewhere we
could go. I never took Eve back to my place in case Chloe
was in, and Eve didn't want us to go to hers because her
mum was home.

Then I remembered the building site. It was set back
from the road, on a quiet part of my route to school. The

builders were hardly ever there and the place was a total dump – just rubble with a few walls and ceilings. It was supposed to be a development of new flats, but they hadn't even started building the first floors yet.

It was private. It was dry. And it was empty. Perfect.

I dragged Eve past the no-entry signs and we huddled there for most of the afternoon.

I tried not to think about her going off with Ben that evening, but it kind of overshadowed our last couple of hours. I knew she was thinking about it too. For once there were no impossible questions.

She got up to leave at about five o'clock, promising me she'd meet me in the same place tomorrow morning. I gave her a long, sad kiss, then padded home in the rain, the whole world muffled and distant.

The house was empty when I got in. It didn't occur to me to wonder where anyone was – I was too wrapped up in my own, numb misery. Chloe crept in through the front door about half an hour later. She jumped when she saw me in the hall.

"I thought you were Mum," she panted, clutching her chest. "I ran all the way. I thought she might have got back early from work."

I shook my head as she pulled off her wet jacket and shoes and shoved them in the back of the hall cupboard.

"Where've you been?" I said.

"Told you," Chloe said, checking her face in the hall mirror. "Out with a friend."

"It's a guy, isn't it?" I said.

Chloe turned to me, smiling. "How about I keep my secrets and you keep yours. Fair?"

I shrugged, wondering again if she'd guessed about me and Eve. She seemed in quite a good mood and talking to her took my mind off Eve and Ben a bit, so I followed her into the kitchen and sat at the table while she made herself a cup of weak, sugary tea.

"Mmmn," she said. "It's pigging freezing out there." She looked at me. "So, things OK?"

"I guess," I said.

"God, you are such an emotional retard." Chloe grinned.

A few weeks ago I'd have been right back at her with some snappy remark. But now my first thought was to wonder if she was right. I mean, it wasn't like Ben was so emotionally mature or anything, but he was seventeen. He could probably do a way-better imitation of being mature than I could. Maybe that was why Eve didn't want to give him up.

"D'you think I'm really immature for my age?"

Chloe laughed. "It's not so much that. More that you don't notice half of what's going on under your nose – like the whole thing with Matt and Mum."

"What thing?" I said.

Chloe nodded. "See. That's what I mean. You've got no idea."

"What? About Mum and Matt?" I said, still not fully understanding.

Chloe rolled her eyes. "Why d'you think he comes round here all the time?"

I shrugged. "To help out? I dunno."

Chloe snorted. "Help himself out, you mean. He's after Mum. You can see it a mile off."

I stared at her. It was true, Matt did come around a lot. But he was always banging on about being Dad's best friend. Surely he wouldn't dream of going after his wife.

"That's disgusting," I said. "D'you think she likes him?"

Chloe nodded. "But she feels guilty because of Dad. And he knows she does, so he's playing it very cool and that's making her even more interested, and then she knows he knows she's interested but no one's saying anything, and it's all building up and sooner or later he'll make his move."

"Has she told you all this?" I asked, bewildered.

"Course not. She only ever talks at me to have a go. But it's obvious."

The front door opened.

"Hi guys," Mum called from the hall.

Chloe put down her mug of tea and moved closer. "Anyway. I'm going out tonight," she whispered. "I won't be back till really late, so I want you to do me this favour. If Mum wonders why my door's locked from the inside again, tell her I had a headache or something and I said I was going to sleep. Don't forget about my headphones being on, either."

But Mum was going out herself. She was dead cagey about it too. "Just a drink and a bite to eat with a friend, Luke, sweetheart. You can sort yourself out some tea, can't you? I'll be back about eleven."

She spent ages getting ready – even asked me how she looked when she came downstairs.

"Nice," I said, suspiciously. God, Chloe was right. Mum was on a date. She left at eight. Chloe slipped out through the front door five minutes later, having locked her bedroom door. I was on my own.

The jealousy kicked in almost immediately. It was like the numb haze of misery lifted and someone stuck a knife in the middle of my chest. My head filled up with these images of Ben and Eve. Kissing. Touching. I knew now that Eve's birthday was next Friday, and my mind was on fast rewind to Ben's words back in the burger bar.

It was a kind of torture. I wandered round the house, the

images of Ben and Eve forcing their way in front of my eyes.

If I'd known where they'd had gone, I think I might have marched down there and punched Ben hard, until he agreed to leave her alone. Well. That was what I fantasised about doing. In the back of my head I knew I wouldn't have really done it. I mean, I might have been obsessed with Eve. But I wasn't stupid.

I paced up and down in my room, getting angrier and angrier. I tried browsing the net, watching TV, listening to music. It was always there in the back of my mind. What was she doing? What was he doing? What was going to happen next?

After a couple of hours I found a half-empty bottle of whisky, left over from Dad's funeral, at the back of one of the kitchen cupboards. I'd unscrewed the top and was on the verge of taking a swig, when a key sounded in the door. "Hi, guys." It was Mum.

Quickly I put the whisky back in the cupboard.

Mum and Matt came into the kitchen. Mum was glowing. Matt looked slightly sheepish.

My fists unclenched. I could feel the rage in my head subsiding and the numb misery sliding back into place.

"Where's Chloe?" Mum smiled.

Oh, crap.

"Up in her room," I lied. "She said she had a headache."

"I'll go and check on her," Mum said. Before I could say anything else, she'd vanished upstairs, leaving me alone in the kitchen with Uncle Matt.

"Just thought I should make sure your mum got home all right," Matt said, gruffly.

I glared at him. "Where d'you take her?" I said.

He looked slightly shocked.

Yeah. I sussed you, you jerk.

The sound of Mum hammering on Chloe's door drifted downstairs towards us. "Let me in, Chloe," Mum was yelling.

Matt muttered something under his breath.

A minute later Mum came flying down the stairs. "Matt, I'm really worried. Luke says she's not well and the door's locked again. She could have collapsed, be lying there unconscious." She gripped his arm. "Oh, God, suppose it's drugs?"

Matt looked at her. "D'you want me to break the door down?"

"Hey, Mum," I said quickly. "There's no need for that. Chloe isn't on drugs. I'm sure of it."

"But she could be really ill in there." Mum twisted her hands together. "Yes, Matt, I think you better had." She and Matt headed upstairs to Chloe's room.

I couldn't believe it. I checked my watch. Ten-forty. Maybe I could call Chloe. If she wasn't too far away, perhaps I could get her to come back right now and somehow sneak into the house unnoticed. I tried her number on my mobile. It went to voicemail.

I started to get worried. Suppose something had happened to Chloe? Maybe this guy she was seeing – this older man Eve reckoned she must be going out with – maybe he'd done something to her.

I went upstairs. Mum and Matt were on the landing outside Chloe's room. Matt was squaring up against the door, his right shoulder turned towards it. He saw me. "Good, Luke. I might need your help for this."

I swallowed. It was quarter to eleven. There was no chance Chloe was inside that room yet.

"Don't bother breaking down the door," I said. "She's not there." They both stared at me.

"What d'you mean, Luke?" Mum said, hoarsely. "Where is she?"

"I don't know," I said. "Honestly. She wouldn't tell me." They went ballistic.

Mostly about Chloe, of course. Though as she wasn't there – and as I had covered up for her again – a lot of the shouting was directed at me.

By midnight, the edge had gone off Mum's anger. In

125

fact, she was starting to get seriously worried. She'd tried Chloe's mobile several times. And she'd rung round all her friends. No one appeared to have any idea where she was.

"Suppose something's happened to her, Matt."

Matt put his arm round Mum's shoulders. Silently I cursed Chloe for creating a situation that was going to give Matt more of a chance to wheedle his way into Mum's life. He'd already done a big heroic number about how he couldn't go home and leave Mum in this state.

Why not? I'm here.

But Mum was pathetically grateful.

I hadn't told Mum anything about the "older guy" theory. But by one o'clock I was wondering if I should. Mum was standing looking out of the living-room window onto the deserted street, biting the skin round her finger-nails, her face ghostly white.

"D'you think I should call the police?" she said.

"Give it a bit longer, love," Matt said soothingly, stroking her hair.

Jesus. He wasn't even pretending not to be interested anymore.

"I can see her," Mum shouted from the window. She ran into the hall and opened the door, just as Chloe sauntered up the path, a bottle of beer in her hand.

Ten seconds later we were in the middle of the worst

row Mum and Chloe had ever had.

"How could you do this to me?" Mum yelled. "I can never, ever trust you again."

"Yeah, big deal. You didn't trust me before. You treat me like a pigging prisoner!" Chloe screamed.

"I don't . . ."

"Yes you do. A prisoner. What d'you expect me to do?"

I watched, helplessly, as they stood, inches away from each other and completely red in the face, shouting at the tops of their voices.

"You hate me. You've always hated me," Chloe shouted, tears splashing down her cheeks.

"I don't hate you," Mum yelled back. "I love you. I care about you. That's why I punish you when you do something dangerous. It's for your—"

"That's pigging bollocks," Chloe screamed. "You just want to ruin my life. Like you ruined Dad's."

Mum blinked. "How dare you talk like that . . . Dad would be so ashamed . . ."

"No, he wouldn't. He loved me. He's what made this a family. Now it's nothing. Nothing."

And with that Chloe turned and fled, hysterically, into her room. Mum moved to go after her, but Matt held her back.

"Don't, love," he said. "Leave her to calm down."

Mum sank, weeping, into his arms.

Excellent.

Severely exasperated with my entire family, I traipsed into my room and flopped onto my bed. I thought about ringing Eve. She had to be home and on her own by now. But I was too scared to call, just in case she wasn't.

In the end, I sat there for hours, staring at Dad's old records. It dawned on me that I hadn't heard the front door shut. Matt wasn't actually staying over was he? In the end I crept onto the landing. Everything was dark and quiet downstairs. Mum's bedroom door was closed and the light inside was off.

I really didn't want to think about that, so I went back into my room and listened to a few of Dad's singles. I recognised a couple. Dad used to play them on CD in the house.

I remembered once finding him and Mum slow-dancing in the kitchen to one of the tracks. Dad had winked at me over her shoulder.

"Nearly lost your mum to this record, Luke," he'd said. "Want to know how I got her back?"

At the time I'd just thought it was gross that they were smooching away in the kitchen. I hadn't taken any notice of what he was saying.

What could he know about how I felt anyway?

I listened to the songs, still sitting on my bed.

Missing Eve.

14

Perfect imperfect

You think you're alone until you realise you're in it.
Now fear is here to stay, love is here for a visit.

'Watching the Detectives'
Elvis Costello and the Attractions

The next day Mum got Uncle Matt to take the lock off Chloe's door so she couldn't shut herself in anymore. She also got him to put a lock *onto* Chloe's window – to which Mum kept the key.

Finally, she extended Chloe's month-long grounding – so that Chloe now had two more weeks of it – and she took Chloe's mobile away.

But it was all pointless. In fact, the only effect of Mum's punishments was that instead of sneaking about, Chloe simply marched in and out of the house whenever she felt like it.

Mum still shouted at her, but now Chloe just ignored her. Literally. She put this vacant look on her face, and acted as if she wasn't even aware Mum was in the room. After a day of this Mum stopped talking to Chloe altogether. She also stopped washing her clothes and cooking her meals. It didn't work.

Chloe simply started doing those things for herself.

I could see Mum was really miserable and I felt angry with Chloe for pushing her so hard. But I didn't know what I could do about it. Chloe's impossible to deal with when she gets angry. Eve said she must be unhappy underneath because of Dad. Maybe. I was sure that if Dad had been here he would have been able to sort her out. But it was way beyond me.

And at least the endless rows had stopped.

I saw Eve the day after her date with Ben. We took a bus into town and went to the movies. I was determined not to mention Ben – but after the film, we went for a coffee and Eve brought him up herself.

"I missed you last night," she said.

"Oh?" I stirred the froth into my cappuccino.

"Ben and I went to this club. It was a great place, but loads of his football friends were there and I don't like them so much. And Ben didn't even want to talk to me properly."

No, I don't suppose he did. I expect he had other things on his mind after being away from you for a week.

Eve sighed. "He's such a weird guy. He's so macho on the outside, but underneath I'm sure there's this vulnerable person he really would rather be, if he'd just let it come through."

Jesus Christ. "Do you mind if we don't talk about Ben anymore?" I snapped. I pushed my coffee away and sat back in my seat.

Eve's lip trembled. "I just wanted you to know that I missed you."

I shook my head. Her logic was all twisted. She was making it sound like someone had forced her to be with Ben last night.

A tear trickled down Eve's face, glistening over the tiny chicken-pox scar she has on the ridge of her cheekbone. And it suddenly struck me that she wasn't perfect. Beautiful and sexy, yes. And kind and funny and sweet and smart.

But she was lots of negative things too. She was stupid about Ben. And annoying – with all her ridiculous questions and the way she was often late when we'd agreed to meet up. And sometimes she was even boring – going on and on about her school stuff or trying to get to the heart of some ultra-complicated emotional point she was making.

The funny thing is, knowing all that only made me want her more.

I smiled at her. " 'S OK," I said. "I missed you too."

Looking back, I can see something changed between us at that moment. I stopped being constantly terrified she was about to dump me. I even found myself forgetting she was older – almost sixteen. It just didn't seem important anymore. I still felt massively jealous that evening, when she went off to be with Ben, but I decided it was crazy to stay in by myself again, so I called Ryan to see what he was doing.

As I suspected he had a party all lined up – and seemed quite happy for me to tag along. There were quite a few people from school there. Everyone seemed to have forgotten about my dad dying – or at least it didn't seem to be such a big deal anymore. I didn't feel everyone was looking at me and thinking: hey, there's Luke with the Dead Dad. In fact, I found myself actually enjoying hanging out with my mates again.

I mean, I would have liked Eve to be there too. But things with her were so intense. What with the powerful way I felt and the whole thing she had going with Ben – it was kind of nice to take a breather.

"So I guess you don't need to know the Sixth and final Step for getting a girl," Ryan said when he saw me. "You've obviously already got her."

I frowned. I hadn't told anyone I'd been seeing Eve. We avoided everywhere we might see people we knew. I'd hardly spoken to anyone else for a week. How did Ryan know about us?

Ryan gave me his lopsided grin. "It's all over your face," he said. "You've been maxing out all half-term, haven't you?"

"Sssh, it's supposed to be a secret." I grimaced. "She's still with her stupid boyfriend. Doesn't want him finding out." A horribly graphic image of Eve and Ben snogging forced its way into my head. I shuddered.

"Ah," Ryan said, looking at me thoughtfully. "Well in that case, the Sixth Step might come in handy. It sounds different from the other Steps, but it's all part of the Masterplan."

I rolled my eyes. *God*. If bullshitting was a GCSE subject, Ryan would already have an A*. "Spit it out, Ry," I snapped.

"OK," he said. "Basically, Step Six is where you go hardcore. You've spent all your time so far focusing on Eve, showing her you're interested, making her laugh, listening. Now you gotta make it clear that you could walk away if you wanted to."

I frowned. "Like being aloof, again?"

Ryan shook his head. "This is different. This is all about saying 'I may be sensitive and stuff, but I'm still a bloke and I've got my pride and I won't put up with any crap'."

He paused. "For instance, you should make it clear you won't put up with her still seeing Ben, as you obviously hate it so much."

"Right." I could feel my face reddening as my temper rose. What did Ryan know about it? Eve had been going out with Ben before she met me. I could hardly demand she dumped him, could I?

I looked round the room, trying to find some way of changing the subject. It was filling up with a crowd of girls I'd never seen before. Some of them were pretty hot. One girl with long, black hair was giving Ryan this hard, sexy stare.

I nudged him. "What you gonna do about *her*?"

He grinned at me, then gazed across the room at the girl. They looked at each other for a few seconds, then Ryan smiled and beckoned her over. "She'll be here in less than a minute," he said confidently. "And she'll bring a friend."

I laughed, but Ryan was right. Thirty seconds later the girl sauntered up to us, a shorter, red-cheeked girl beside her.

"Hi," said Ryan. He raised his eyebrows and smiled.

The dark-haired girl started talking to him as if me and the other girl weren't there. Ryan flirted right back at her. Then the girl said she was going to get a drink. We all watched her as she crossed the room. She turned at the door and stared straight at Ryan. Then she walked out.

"See you later, man." Without looking at me, Ryan strolled out after the girl.

I turned to her friend. She was smiling shyly up at me. She looked nice. She was even quite pretty. But she wasn't Eve. I considered getting off with her for about ten seconds. Why shouldn't I?

It was probably what Eve was doing right now.

Then my phone rang. It was a text from Eve. i miss u.

"Sorry," I said to the girl. "Gotta go."

I walked round for a bit, chatting to some people I knew. I kept an eye out for Ryan, but I didn't see him anywhere. He was probably happily snogging the dark-haired girl in some corner.

I left him to it and went home.

Eve was furious when I told her about the party and the shy girl the next day.

"So while I'm missing you like mad, all you're thinking about is who you can pull?" she said indignantly.

I couldn't help smiling. "I told you, nothing happened."

"Only 'cause I texted you and reminded you . . . Why are you laughing at me?"

I pulled her into a massive snog. "Because you're jealous," I said, grinning my head off. "Because you're jealous."

It was Sunday, the last day before we went back to school and we were on our own at Eve's house. It was still morning, and the whole day stretched ahead of us. We'd made some sandwiches and were eating them lying on the sofa. We were just talking about what we should do later, when the doorbell rang.

I watched Eve glide across the hall and open the door.

I couldn't see who was there.

"Ben," she said, loudly.

I practically choked on the bit of sandwich I'd just put into my mouth.

"What are you doing here?" Eve's voice sounded far too nervous and high-pitched. *Jesus.* He was going to guess something was up.

I could hear Ben grunting about how his football practice had finished early as I rolled off the sofa onto the floor. My eyes flashed up to the window at the front of the house. Could he see into the living room from where he was standing?

"Why can't I come in?" he said suspiciously.

Oh my God. I glanced round and spotted a big squashy armchair in the corner by the window. I set off on my hands and knees towards it.

"I've got to go out in a minute," Eve said. "I told you I'm seeing my dad."

I could hear them arguing as I wriggled past a tall floor lamp and crawled behind the chair. The curtain at the window beside me hung right to the floor. I tugged at the folds so they hid me fully, then peeked through a tiny slit.

They were in the living-room doorway. Ben was swearing, pushing past Eve. He took in the sandwiches – luckily we'd shared a single plate – then he stomped further into the room.

I held my breath.

"So when are you seeing your dad?" Ben growled.

Eve shrank against the wall. I knew she had pretended her dad was visiting this weekend.

"A bit later. His flight from Spain's . . . er . . . about to land."

A lecherous grin spread across Ben's face. "So we've got a bit of time, then?"

"No." Eve was practically squeaking now, all trace of her normally raspy voice completely gone. "I've got to get ready. Now."

Ben pulled her towards him. "You know you want me." He pawed at Eve's dress.

I gritted my teeth.

She pushed him away. "No," she said firmly. "I'll see you tomorrow."

After a little more argument, Ben allowed himself to be

propelled towards the door. This was followed by a few minutes of slurping noises which I tried not to listen to. Then he was gone.

Eve came back into the living room as I stood up. We stared at each other for a few seconds. I was about to start mouthing off about what a total jerk Ben was, when she started crying.

We sat down on the sofa and I put my arms round her. I had no idea what to say. I couldn't stop thinking about the way Ben had touched her. I hated it. Not just seeing his hands on her body. It was his whole attitude. He'd acted like he owned her.

Eve wiped her eyes. "What are you thinking?" she said.

The most irritating question in the world again. But for once I wanted to answer. "I don't understand . . ." I said, slowly, ". . . why you go out with him. Why you let him 'do stuff'?"

Eve wrinkled her nose. "We don't really 'do' anything. I mean, not like you and me."

I frowned. What was she talking about? Everything I'd seen of Ben so far made it quite clear to me that getting as far as he could with Eve was his main reason for hanging out with her.

"It's like, with us, we spend lots of time talking and stuff and it's really nice," she said. "But with Ben, it's more complicated. I really . . . I mean, he's fun to be with. We go out with his mates . . . you know to clubs and bars and . . . and I have a good time. But we don't talk that much . . . you know . . . not that he gets all stressy about anything. I mean he'd never *make* me do anything I didn't want to. He says he's totally cool about waiting for . . . until I'm ready . . ."

I shook my head. It was all too complicated. Too hard to make sense of. Somewhere in my head a little voice was insisting that Ryan was right. I shouldn't ignore Step Six. I should make Eve dump Ben.

But it was a very little voice. And, after all, I had Eve.

That was all that mattered.

We met every day that week after school – mostly in the building site. Some workmen had obviously been in there, because another bit of wall had appeared, but no one was ever around by the time we turned up.

Thursday was after-school Art Club. I had confessed to Eve some time ago how I'd only started going in order to talk to her. She told me I should do the wooden-button music collage anyway. That it was a good idea. Privately, I thought she was nuts, but I didn't say anything.

I was looking forward to after Club ended, when we'd

agreed we would stay on late again. It was going to be one of the few opportunities I had to be with Eve indoors – i.e. in a place where she wasn't wearing ten layers of jumpers and coats.

As soon as Ms Patel had left we switched the radio on. This time *I* found some music. Slow-dance music.

As the song finished, I pulled away from her and drew a small, tissue-wrapped package out of my pocket.

"Happy birthday," I said.

Eve looked up – all wide-eyed and smiling. Her birthday was the next day, but, of course, she would be going out with Ben and her friends. Which meant I wouldn't see her until Saturday.

She unwrapped the package eagerly.

I held my breath, hoping she was going to like it. I'd bought her a silver necklace with pale blue stars hanging from it. It was a bit like one Chloe had.

"It's beautiful," Eve breathed.

I grinned, relieved, as she rushed to the mirror to put it on. The necklace rested prettily against her skin. She raced back. "I'll try and call you tomorrow night." She hugged me, her eyes shining. "Promise."

I'd already made plans to go out the next night with Ry and a few other friends. We went bowling and then for a burger. It was fun, though from time to time I couldn't help wondering what Eve was doing. Ryan noticed me staring at my phone a couple of times.

"Waiting for a call?" he said.

I shrugged. "Maybe."

"Let's hope it's not a relegation announcement," Ryan grinned. "You know, from the Premiership."

I threw my burger wrapper at him. He ducked and it landed in a cup of coffee belonging to some old guy at the next table.

The old guy jumped up, shouting at us, and promptly knocked over the drinks of these two girls sitting opposite him.

Ryan and I were laughing so much at the horrified expression on his face that I nearly missed my ring tone. Then, when I finally heard it, I lunged for it so fast that I knocked it off the table. Ryan hooted with laughter as I disappeared underneath, scrabbling on the ground.

It was a text.

mt m @ site x

I frowned. Eve was normally a bit more flowery with her texts than that. And she'd never asked me to meet her so late before. Still, maybe she didn't have much time when she wrote it. Maybe she was hating being out with Ben and her friends. I smiled to myself.

Ryan raised his eyebrows. "Good news?"

"Yeah." I reached for my jacket. "I gotta go."

It took me ten minutes to get to the building site. I realised as I stepped over the low chain that the no-entry sign hung from, that I didn't know whether Eve was already there – or still on her way.

I stumbled around for a bit, calling her name out softly. I knew the site quite well now, but in the pitch black it was hard to see where the rubble-strewn ground rose and fell. I reached the most built-up part of the site, where a short stretch of breeze-block was divided into rooms with walls and ceilings and holes for windows. I peered inside the first room. It was dark. Creepy.

I couldn't imagine Eve could possibly be waiting inside, but then, maybe she'd have felt safer there than out by the front where passers-by could see her. "Eve?" I said.

Something rustled in the far corner.

"Eve. Is that you?"

I took a step inside. The darkness seemed almost to pulsate as my eyes strained into it. And then I sensed movement behind me.

I spun round, just as someone grabbed my arm.

15

Beaten

I first felt a fist
And then a kick
I could now smell their breath
They smelled of pubs

'Down in the Tube Station at Midnight'
The Jam

Everything seemed to happen at once.

A light shone in my eyes. Blinding me. The hand on my arm tightened its grip. Someone else grabbed the other arm. There were grunts. Shouts. I was being pulled backwards, dragged along the concrete floor towards the back of the breeze-block room.

My heart pounded furiously, right up in my throat. I wanted to yell out, but my voice was trapped somewhere deep in my head. I tried to pull away from the hands that held my arms. But they dug in harder.

And then the light dropped and I looked up, blinking, trying to adjust to the darkness.

My throat tightened. Ben was standing in front of me. His face was twisted with fury – every muscle tensed, teeth bared, eyes wild.

"You little shit," he yelled.

Wham. His fist rammed into my stomach.

It was like all the air had been sucked out of me. I doubled over, pain radiating out from my belly. The two guys on either side of me jerked me upright. I turned instinctively towards one of them, my eyes pleading for them to let me go. But he was looking at Ben.

Wham. Ben's fist drove even deeper into me. I gasped for breath. Again, the two guys holding my arms pulled me upright. I dimly registered who they were – Ben's friends from the burger bar I'd overheard all those weeks ago.

Then Ben shoved his face right up in front of mine. He grabbed my hair. Yanked my head right back. He leaned right over me. "She's *mine*, you disgusting little jerk."

He spat on my face. Just under my eye. A glob of wetness rolled down my cheek. Then he let go of my head. Stepped back. Punched. *Smack.* Right into my jaw. My nose. His fist smashing into me. Over and over.

I couldn't breathe. I was nothing except the pain driving

against my face. This low moaning started. It took me a few seconds to realise it was my own voice. Then the hands holding me up let go. I collapsed onto the floor.

I tried to push myself up, but my arms and legs were shaking too much. I sank back against the concrete. The pain in my face was agony.

Above my head, laughter. "Not such a pretty-boy now."

A boot came out of nowhere, glancing off my ribs. A half-hearted kick. Not Ben's. I curled up on the floor, covering my head with my arms, knowing they hadn't finished.

More kicks pounded against my arms and legs. I was only pain. Only fear. Lying there, waiting for it to end. And then it did. I lay there panting for a few seconds, then lifted up my arm and looked up. A boot was poised, ready to ram into my jaw. I stared at it and everything slowed down. I had time to think, with absolute certainty, that if that boot connected with my face I was going to die.

"Stop, Ben."

"That's enough."

Beyond the boot, I could see Ben's two mates pulling him away from me. Shouting. Ben's yells drowning out the others. And then he was back, bending down over me. I braced myself. This was it. I was dead.

But he was pushing my arms off my face, forcing my mouth open, ramming something metallic past my lips, wet with blood.

His beery breath suddenly hot on my cheek. "You ever go near her again and I'll kill you," he shouted. Then he drew closer, his voice lowered menacingly. "Tell anyone I did this and I'll kill *her*."

Then he stood up, turned away. They were gone.

I lay there, unable to move, unable to think. I spat the metal chain out of my mouth. It was the silver necklace with the pale blue stars I had given Eve.

Every part of my body throbbed with pain. My mind shut down. I couldn't focus on anything else other than the pain. Then everything went black.

I don't know how long I was out for. I came to several times, registering something ringing near me. I dimly knew it was a phone, that someone should answer it. Once I tried to move, but everything hurt and I couldn't work out where to put my hands to push myself up and I collapsed back down into the darkness.

The next time I came round, my left eye was all swollen up. I could hardly see out of it. The pain had subsided a little, but I was cold. My whole body was shaking with it. It occurred to me that I ought to shout for help or something. But I couldn't make my voice work.

Then I heard footsteps running towards me.

"Ryan, Ryan. Oh Jesus. He's here." It was Chloe's voice. That didn't make sense. What was she doing here?

She knelt over me, her eyes wide. "Oh God, Luke. Oh my God."

I tried to speak to her, but my mouth still wouldn't work properly. Chloe pulled me up against her. I could feel the warmth of her body through my jacket. She was pulling her coat off, putting it round my shoulders. Then Ryan was there too. Standing above me, his long fringe hanging over his upside-down eyes.

"Look at his face," Chloe was saying. "Look what they've done to him."

"Shit." Ryan squatted down in front of me. "We've got to get him out of here. Hey, Luke, man. It's gonna be OK."

He reached out and put his hands under my armpits. He tried to pull me away from Chloe, and upright. But I was shaking too hard to take any of my own weight. As I moved, pain filled my body again. A wave of nausea rolled up through me. I groaned and puked over Ryan's shoes.

He jumped back, letting me sag back against Chloe. "Jesus."

"Call an ambulance." Chloe's voice was panicky, urgent. "He's cold as ice. Hurry."

I leaned deep against her. She wrapped both arms around me and rocked me gently. "It's going to be all right, it is, Luke – oh please let it be all right."

I could hear her sobbing as Ryan spoke on the phone.

"Eve?" I whispered.

Chloe leaned forwards. "What is it, Luke?"

"Eve?" I was trying to ask if she was OK. But all I could manage was her name.

"Yeah, she called me. I called Ryan. Don't think about it now, Luke. Everything's going to be OK."

I couldn't work out what any of it meant. I was so cold. The shaking was getting worse.

Ryan flicked his phone shut. "They'll be here in a minute." He squatted back down in front of me. "It was Ben, wasn't it? Was he on his own?"

"No way," I tried to smile at him, to indicate there had been an army attacking me, but I felt sick again. I looked down. Why couldn't I make my body stop trembling?

Chloe was stroking my hair. Like Mum used to when I was little. Ben's last words suddenly flashed back into my head. I looked up at Ryan.

"Ry," I whispered hoarsely.

"What, mate?"

I made a superhuman effort to speak through my chattering teeth. "Don't tell. 'Bout Eve. 'Bout Ben."

Ryan frowned. I could see him look up above my head to Chloe.

"Please," I said. "Don't say . . . Ben."

"OK, man, whatever. We won't say anything. Don't talk anymore."

Satisfied, I lay back against Chloe and let the darkness take me.

When I woke up, the pain and the shaking were gone. I was warm, lying under crisp, smooth sheets. I could tell it was light in the room through the glare against my eyelids. People were murmuring in low voices in the distance.

I opened my eyes. The left one was just a narrow slit, but through the other I could see Mum, in a chair next to me. Her face was stained with tear tracks. She squeezed my hand. "Oh my God, my baby, my baby."

I wrinkled my nose. "Mu-um." It came out in this hoarse whisper. I swallowed. There was no pain anymore, but my whole body ached.

"Where am I?" I said.

"Hospital. Chloe and your friend Ryan brought you here in an ambulance. They're still here, down in the cafeteria." She smiled at me. "I was just talking to the doctor. She says you're very lucky. There's nothing broken and no internal injuries. Just lots of cuts and bruises."

I frowned at her. "What time is it?"

"About one or so. Lunchtime. You've been asleep for hours. Oh, Luke, when you didn't come home . . ." Mum paused, gulping back her tears. I tried to squeeze her hand, but the effort made me feel sick.

"Did you see who did this?" Mum said. "Did you know them?"

I shook my head, then closed my eyes and sank back against the pillows.

The next time I woke up, the pain was worse in my face, but I felt less exhausted. And I was starving. I could see I was in a long ward, with beds in two rows opposite each other. Mum was talking to one of the nurses by the door.

"Hey. Babe-magnet."

I focused on the figure at the end of the bed. It was Chloe. She was munching on a sandwich, grinning at me.

"How you feeling?" she said.

"Can I have some of your sandwich?" I said.

Chloe walked over and handed me the remainder of her sandwich. I bit into it hungrily. "Ow." My jaw hurt to move. I chewed more slowly.

"Tell me what happened," Chloe said, sitting down beside me.

I explained briefly as much as I could remember. "You haven't said anything have you?" I asked anxiously, glancing over at Mum. "Ben said if I told anyone he'd . . . he'd hurt Eve."

Chloe shook her head. "Me and Ryan talked to the police last night. We just said we got worried when you didn't get home, so we went to look for you."

Chloe explained how she'd been out at some party when she'd got a call from Eve. "It wasn't that late. Before eleven. She was hysterical – said that Ben was coming after you. Apparently he'd taken her phone and sent you some text on it, pretending to be from her?"

I nodded.

"She said something about her birthday. How she and Ben were going out, how she couldn't call earlier. Frankly it didn't make sense. Anyway, I knew you were out with Ryan so I got hold of him and he said we should go round the places you and Eve met. So we did."

I put down my sandwich. "Did you know before?" I said. "About Eve?"

"Yeah, I kind of worked it out a while back," Chloe smiled. "But I thought I'd be cool and keep my nose out."

I smiled back, then sat up, determined to get out of bed.

"Hey. Slow down. D'you want me to call her? Eve?" Chloe said. "Make sure she's OK?"

"I gotta see her," I said, swinging my legs off the bed.

I looked down. I was wearing one of those hospital

gowns that do up round the back. Below my knees my shins were a mass of bruises.

"Man," I said.

"Wait till you see your face," Chloe grinned. She fished in her handbag and pulled out a little mirror.

I looked into it. *Jesus*. The whole left side of my face was red and swollen. You could hardly see the eye. The skin was broken in several places and held together with little white strips. My lip was swollen and cut too. Altogether I looked a mess.

Mum came bustling over. "Lie back down, Luke. You're not going anywhere."

"But . . .?"

"No buts. That's final."

In the end they let me out that evening.

I tried to call Eve on her mobile a couple of times, but it was always switched off. Chloe rang Eve's house for me, but her mum said she was out.

I guessed that must at least mean she was OK.

For the first time since he died I found myself really wishing Dad was here. I could have told him everything, I reckoned. He would have known what to do. I mean, Mum was just too much of . . . of a mum. If I explained to her what had really happened, she'd only worry and fuss over me even more. And she would never understand how much

I hated Ben. How much I longed to get him back for what he'd done.

In the end, I told the police I'd been jumped by three strangers. No idea what they looked like.

What else could I do? Ben's final words rang in my head. I'd seen his face. I knew what he was capable of.

I was afraid for Eve.

Mum wanted me to stay off school on Monday, but there was no way I wasn't going in. I had to see her. Make sure she was OK.

I took some painkillers to ease the aching in my jaw, and set off. I knew I looked like my face had been turned inside out. I was braced for people to stare at me.

But I was not expecting what happened next.

16

Lies

In the morning I awake
My arms, my legs, my body aches
The sky outside is wet and grey
So begins another weary day.
So begins another weary day.
After eating I go out
People passing by me shout
I can't stand this agony,
Why don't they talk to me?

'Grey Day
Madness

As I entered the classroom, the talking stopped. Everyone turned round and stared at me.

Embarrassed, I scurried to my desk.

I buried my face in my bag and made a big show of digging out last week's homework. I knew when I looked up people would be crowding round, eager to find out all the gory details of what had happened to me. I'd decided to repeat the story I'd given Mum and the police. Hopefully after a couple of hours everyone would forget about it – and maybe at break I could go and find Eve.

I looked up. No one was there. In fact, it was as if people had deliberately moved away from me – they all had their backs turned, concentrating on other things. There was this low-level tension in the air.

I stared round. To be honest I was a bit hurt. I mean, I hadn't wanted to be the centre of attention, everyone staring at my messed-up face. But I had at least expected my mates to show a bit of concern.

I wandered over to the guys I sometimes played football with.

One of them – a tall, skinny guy called Jamie – caught my eye. He folded his arms. "So did you really do it?"

"Do what?" I could feel everyone was now watching me.

Jamie looked uncomfortable. "What Ben says you did."

I stood there, my face flushing. What the hell was going on? Ben had demanded I say nothing. That he would kill Eve if I did.

"What did Ben say?" I said, cautiously.

Some of the girls were crowding round now. One of them sniggered.

"You know." Jamie's cheeks were scarlet. "About with Eve?"

Oh, God. I knew it didn't matter what I said, my face was giving me away. I lowered my eyes.

"Shit." Jamie sounded disgusted. "If it was my girl-friend, you'd have had worse."

I stared at him. Was he really saying that my having seen Eve behind Ben's back a few times justified what Ben had done to me?

Jamie turned his back on me.

I wandered across the room to my desk again. The atmosphere was stretched taut. I could practically feel people hating me.

Leaving my bag behind, I left the room. I couldn't wait until break. I had to see Eve, find out what was going on. As I walked along the corridor towards her classroom my heart pounded. I still needed to be careful when I saw her – not make anything too obvious until I knew exactly what was happening. I thought it through. Best thing was to go in, go up to Chloe. Try and speak to her privately.

I opened the door to Eve and Chloe's classroom and peered inside. At first nobody noticed me – they were all talking too loudly. Lots of people were crowded round Eve's desk. I couldn't even see if she was there. I glanced

156

across the room at Chloe. She was waving her arms, clearly telling me to go away. I pointed to where Eve sat, holding my hands up questioningly. *What's going on?*

"I don't believe it," said a deep voice beside me. I spun round, and came face to face with a thickset boy I didn't know. He was sneering at me, his beefy hands rounded into fists.

My heart started pounding.

"Show your face anywhere near here again and I'll make it look even worse than it does now," he growled.

I backed out of the door and leaned against the wall in the corridor. Tears pricked at my eyes. My hands were shaking. That deep, menacing voice had taken me straight back to Friday night.

And yet this was almost worse.

I understood why Ben was mad with me. I'd gone after his girlfriend. But why was the entire school angry? My fear mutated to rage. It wasn't fair. I was the one who'd been left in a bleeding pulp.

Chloe appeared at my shoulder, her forehead wrinkled with concern. "Get out of here," she hissed.

"What the hell is happening?" I said, clenching my fists.

"It's Eve. They all think you attacked her."

"What?"

Chloe pushed me away from the wall, prodding me

along the corridor, back in the direction of my own class-room. "Ben is saying that he only beat you up because you tried to force Eve to . . . you know . . . He says he caught you attacking her."

"But that's rubbish. Why doesn't everyone just ask Eve?"

Chloe lowered her eyes. "Eve says it's true."

I stared at her. The corridor seemed to spin round my head. For a second I thought I was going to pass out again. I leaned against the wall.

Eve was telling lies about me?

Chloe prodded me forwards. "Go away."

I stood my ground. There had to be some reason Eve would make up a story like that. It didn't make sense. The bell rang.

"Can't you tell them it's not true?"

"I have," Chloe sighed. "But they don't believe me. They think I'm just sticking up for you because you're my brother."

"I'm going to talk to Eve," I said, heading back towards her classroom door. "There's got to be some mistake. She can't do this."

Chloe clutched at my arm. "Don't be ridiculous. Eve's really popular, especially with all the guys in our class. There are several of them in there right now who would happily break both your legs if you go anywhere near her. Leave it. At least for now."

I hesitated, knowing that Chloe was right. There was no point me trying to talk to Eve at the moment. The bell had gone and there were too many people around.

I turned round, a huge lump in my throat. Chloe patted me on the back. "Forget her," she said. "She's not worth it."

When I got back to my classroom I found someone had emptied the contents of my bag into the rubbish bin.

I picked everything out and trudged back to my desk.

I sent another text and left my phone switched on all day, but Eve didn't ring.

The more I thought about it, the more I was sure there could only be one reason for the lies she was telling about me.

Ben had forced her to choose between me and him. And she had chosen him.

When I got home that day I told Mum that my face hurt and that maybe I'd gone back to school a bit early.

She agreed I could stay off the rest of the week.

17

Tempted

Yesterday I got so old
I felt like I could die
Yesterday I got so old
It made me want to cry

'In-between Days'
The Cure

By Wednesday evening my eye had gone back to its original size and the bruising on my face had turned from dark red to a purply shade of yellow.

My heart, on the other hand, was still ripped to pieces.

Ryan came round after school. He told me he'd spent the whole day telling people Ben and Eve were making their story up.

"Everyone who knows you believes me now, which takes care of most of our year." He shook his head. "Be easier if Eve wasn't going round school crying, though."

I gritted my teeth, tasting the bitterness in my mouth. I was glad she was upset. She deserved to be.

Later that evening Uncle Matt turned up for a meal. Chloe ate with us for once – I think Mum had asked her to for my sake. She and Mum had been getting on a bit better since I'd been beaten up and it was obvious they were both making an effort to avoid another row.

It was nice of them – but I didn't care what they did.

I sat at the kitchen table, staring at my plate while the others chatted about boring work and school stuff. Mum tried to get me to talk for a while, then she gave up and left me picking at my food.

After we'd eaten, Mum gave this nervous little cough.

"Matt and I wanted to tell you both something."

I glanced at Chloe.

"We know, Mum." Chloe rolled her eyes. "We've known for ages. The two of you are an Item."

"There's no need to talk to your mum like that," Matt snapped.

I stared back at my plate.

Mum took Matt's hand and laid it on the table, his fingers linked with her own. "Come on, guys, I don't want a fight. I wanted you two to be the first we told. What do you think?"

"I think it's a bit quick," Chloe said. "Dad only died two months ago."

Mum nodded. "I agree. That's why we're going to take it slowly. No one's doing anything dramatic. Luke?"

I could feel Mum's eyes boring into me. I looked up.

"Whatever," I said.

I got up and went next door to the living room. Dad's ashes were in their wooden box on the mantelpiece, exactly where I had told Mum to put them. Dad's dead body. In Dad's dead house.

It hadn't done any good.

Matt was going to come in and try and sweep all traces of Dad away. Mum was betraying Dad, just as Eve had betrayed me.

I fixed my eyes on the wooden box.

Sorry, Dad. I'm sorry this is happening.

The doorbell rang. I could hear Chloe at the door, muttering angrily to someone. I attempted a weak smile. Whatever duster and dishcloth salesman had happened round tonight hadn't bargained on Chloe in a bad mood.

Then I caught a snatch of what she was saying.

"Bloody slag. Making up stories about him. Pig off out of here. He can do miles better than you."

I rushed into the hall. "Chlo," I snapped.

She sucked in her breath and stood back.

Eve was standing in the doorway. Her lips were slightly parted, as if she was about to speak.

My stomach did a back flip.

How could her face be so beautiful when her heart was so rotten?

Chloe backed out of the way, still muttering. She stomped up the stairs.

I went over to the door. "What do you want?"

Eve's eyes were darting over my face, taking in my bruises. She reached out her hand to touch my cheek.

"Don't touch me." I took a step back.

Eve whipped her hand back. Her eyes filled with tears.

"I wanted to talk to you," she said.

"Go on."

"Can't I come in?"

I shrugged and let her walk past me.

Mum wandered into the hall. "Hi, Eve," she said, distractedly. "You'll find Chloe in her room."

I followed Eve up the stairs. Silently I led her into my room and shut the door.

Eve sat on the bed and looked round. I stared at her, remembering how I'd once wanted her in here with me more than anything. And now she was here. And it was all spoiled.

She pointed to the cardboard box of singles in the corner. "Are those your dad's records?" she said.

"What do you want?"

"To tell you what happened," Eve's voice was almost a whisper.

I said nothing.

"That night, on my birthday," Eve said, "Ben told me to meet round at his before we went out. When I got there he said now I was sixteen maybe we could . . . you know . . . take our relationship to the next level."

"I don't want to hear—"

"Wait," Eve said. "I said no. I said I wasn't ready. That he was going too fast. And he got angry. He noticed my necklace and asked where it came from. I didn't lie very well about it and he could see I was all nervy. Then he ripped it off and grabbed my phone and started going through the sent and saved texts. He saw your name coming up and asked me who you were."

"And you told him, just like that?"

"No. I didn't tell him anything. But he guessed. He guessed the whole thing. I know you think Ben's stupid, but he's not. He knew someone was at my house the other day – when it was you. And that came up again. And he went on and on, yelling at me. And there was no point denying it anymore."

"Right."

"I said you and I were just friends. That we did the after-school Art Club together. At first I thought he'd believed

164

me. We went out for my birthday, had a pizza with some of my friends and he was . . ." she glanced at me, ". . . he seemed nice, you know? But he still had my phone and I wanted to call you, so I asked for it back. But he said no. And then he got really mean and . . . and he called me these horrible names. And then I knew he was going to come after you. I tried to get away, so I could warn you. But he made me come with him to the park." Eve started sobbing. "And then he sent you some text I didn't see. And he told me he was going to kill you. And then he left me and I ran as hard as I could until I came to a phone box that worked. But it took ages. And I called you, but you didn't answer. And then I called Chloe. I didn't care about anyone finding out about us anymore. I just wanted you to be safe. And I'm so . . . so sorry that he hurt you."

She put her head in her hands and wept.

I stared at her, for once unmoved by her tears.

"What about afterwards?" My voice shook. "When you told the whole school that I'd attacked you? Like I was some disgusting, out-of-control pervert that you only just managed to get away from."

"D'you think I *wanted* to say that?" Eve stood up and strode towards me, her palms open at her sides. "Ben's stupid mates couldn't keep their mouths shut. They started boasting about beating you up. I think Ben realised that if it got out I'd been seeing someone two years younger than he is, he'd look stupid. So he made up this story about how you'd tried it on with me, how you wouldn't take no for an answer and how – thanks to him – I only just managed to get away. He knew that then he'd look like a hero and that everyone would hate you."

She stood in front of me, her eyes pleading with me to understand.

I wanted so much just to lean forwards and kiss her mouth. *No.* I clenched my fists. I wasn't going to let her make a fool of me again.

"And how exactly did Ben 'make' you go along with his stupid story?"

Eve stared at me, as if surprised I didn't already know the answer.

"He said if I didn't back up what he said, he'd come after you again. And this time it would be just him and he would hurt you much, much worse. I was scared, Luke. I was trying to protect you."

I closed my eyes. Eve was right. Ben *was* clever. Clever enough to use how Eve and I felt about each other to get exactly what he wanted from both of us.

Eve leaned against me, then stretched up and brushed her lips gently across my bruised cheek. "I've missed you so much," she whispered. "I was scared to call. I didn't think

166

you'd ever want to see me again. But now we can go back to how it was." She reached up and hooked her arm gently round my neck. "I know it's risky but . . . but we've just got to be more careful. Make sure Ben doesn't find out."

My heart started racing as she drew me into a long, slow kiss. I could feel myself falling down, down into her.

Then I came to my senses. *Step Six. Don't take any crap.*

"No." I pushed her away. "Ben threatened me too. Said he'd kill *you* if I told anyone he'd beaten me up. So I didn't tell. But I was wrong. And you're wrong too."

"But if I don't back him up he'll—"

"Ben's full of shit. He's not really going to kill either of us." I remembered something Ryan had once said. "All Ben cares about is looking good in front of his mates. He doesn't want you particularly. He just doesn't want you to dump him, especially for someone younger. I bet if you made it look mutual, he'd find someone else and wouldn't care what you did."

I walked over to the window. The sky was a dull grey over the rooftops opposite.

"I think Ben's a jerk. And I think he went way too far in what he did to me. But you know what? I don't blame him for being angry with me. You're his girlfriend. If I was him, I'd have been angry too."

I lowered my gaze to the porch roof of the house across

the road. Why did Eve want to be with Ben anyway? I suddenly realised how little respect I had for that. How little respect I had for myself if I accepted it.

I turned round, praying she would understand.

"You have to choose, Eve. Him or me. You can't have both."

She stared at me for a few seconds, her face unreadable. Then she turned and walked out of my room.

18

Other girls

I'll go back and pick another girl, again.
Close my eyes 'cause I know they're all the same
At the love parade

'The Love Parade'
The Undertones

I was dreading going back to school on Monday, but in the
end it wasn't too bad. A few people in other years were
still a bit weird, but my actual class were all really friendly.
Jamie even came up to me and apologised for misunder-
standing what had happened.

"Not that I'm saying you were right to go out with
someone else's girlfriend," he said, cautiously, "but Ben
was way out of order hurting you like that."

Even allowing for the fact that gossip in school always
moves on quickly, I knew that Ryan must have used every

ounce of persuasive charm he could muster to change people's minds about me so fast.

I tried to thank him, but he got all gruff and embarrassed.

"What are mates for?" he said.

I shook my head. I was sure there had to be more to it than that. Ryan had put his own popularity on the line in order to stand up for me. That was an act beyond casual friendship.

Not for the first time, I wondered why he was always so eager to help me.

I never saw Ben. The sixth form were in a different building, so the only place we were ever likely to meet was the cafeteria.

I started taking a packed lunch.

I thought about going to the police – telling them what had really happened. But I couldn't bear the thought of going back over it again. I wasn't even sure they'd believe me. My guess was they'd be all suspicious, all *you've changed your tune, son* about it. And, in the end, it would be my word against Ben's – who would have two friends to back up whatever story he came up with.

A couple of weeks passed. I dropped out of Art Club, but I still saw Eve in the distance from time to time. I told myself I didn't care about her anymore.

I was lying.

Chloe could see how I felt and took a typically hard line. "Stay away from her," she said. "You're better off without her."

She and Mum had stopped shouting at each other for almost a week after I got beaten up. But now the rows had started again – worse than ever.

And when Mum wasn't yelling at Chloe, she was trying to involve me in these massively embarrassing conversations about her and Matt.

"It's not like I'm rushing into anything, Luke," she'd say. "But Dad was so ill for so long, that it was almost like I did a lot of my mourning before he died."

I didn't know what to say to her.

I didn't like Matt. That was that.

I spent most of my time either alone or with Ryan. He made me laugh. And had a far more positive attitude to me and Eve splitting up than Chloe. It was less to do with Eve, in fact, and more to do with getting me over her.

"We gotta pick up the old Six Steps," he kept saying. "Get you a new babe."

After spending two weekends in a row just moping about the house, I finally agreed to go to a party with him. Tones – now a serious item with Kirsty – had invited Ryan to Kirsty's cousin's party on Saturday night.

171

"She's hot," Ryan informed me. "The cousin, I mean. I've seen pictures. There'll be loads of cool people there and Tones has only told me from our year – so none of the girls'll know that you're a sex maniac and likely to attack them as soon as they get within half a metre of you."

"Ha, ha." I made a face at him, shrugging to indicate I could take or leave the party. But the truth was I'd been miserable for so long, I was ready for some fun.

And the party turned out to be awesome. Kirsty's cousin's parents were away for the weekend, but they lived in this massive house, on the edge of town, with the nearest neighbours miles away. The music was loud and wild and, best of all, there were far more girls there than boys.

I'd just had my hair cut again and the bruises on my face had practically disappeared. I felt pretty confident as we wandered into the open-plan living room.

Ryan was always fun to be with. He made me practise his stupid 'look' on a couple of the girls in the first group we saw. But one just stared blankly back at me, and the other asked me pointedly if there was something wrong with my eyesight.

"It's no good," I said to Ryan, my confidence dwindling fast, "I can't do it like you."

It only worked with Eve – and when I wasn't trying.

But then Tones bounded up, his arm, as usual, clamped round Kirsty's waist. He and Ryan started chatting about something, and Kirsty beckoned to me to bend down so she could whisper in my ear.

I had to bend down quite far, because Kirsty's pretty short – and Kirsty ended up shouting because the music was so loud. But what she was saying was clear enough. One of her cousin's friends thought I was cute. Would I like to talk to her?

"Sure." I let Kirsty lead me out into the hall.

"This is Ella." Kirsty grinned, nodding at a slim girl wearing a short, black dress. She vanished back to Tones, leaving us alone.

"Hi." I smiled.

It was easy enough to talk to Ella. She was friendly and pretty and – thanks to the Six Steps – I knew exactly what I was doing with her. I chatted for a bit, asking who she knew at the party and where she went to school. Then I went for my Angle.

"So you gotta have a boyfriend, no?"

Ella blushed a little. "Why d'you say that?"

I let my eyes linger on her face. "You know," I said. "Looking like you do." I tilted my head to one side and glanced up and down her body – just a short, appreciative look.

Ella edged a little closer. She looked up at me coyly. "And how do I look?"

"Mmmn," I said, moving in for the kill. "Like a model."

Ten seconds later we were snogging our heads off.

It must have been about half an hour later that I saw her.

Ella had gone off to the bathroom and I was standing in the hall watching Ryan chat up three girls simultaneously.

I felt someone brushing past me and I looked round. I caught a flash of sleek blonde hair, then it disappeared into the crowd. I pushed forwards through the people, searching for her.

There she was. Going up the stairs. I barged my way onto the stairs and fought past all the couples making out on the lower steps. About halfway up I caught up with her.

I reached out my hand. Touched her shoulder. "Eve?"

She turned round.

Not Eve. A longer face, darker blue eyes. Not anything like Eve.

"Sorry," I mumbled. "I thought you were someone I knew."

I made my way slowly back down the stairs. All the fun seemed to have been sucked out of the party. I felt tears of anger prick at my eyes. I hated Eve for spoiling every little thing I tried to do. I'd tried to turn myself into ice. And Eve had somehow found a way to break through even that.

Ryan came up to me as I fought my way back through the hall. "Me and Tones are getting the last tube home," he said. "D'you wanna come?"

I looked around. "Where's your hot chick for the night then?" I said, not all that bitterly, considering.

Ryan shrugged. "I'm meeting someone later."

I stared at him. "Later?" It was already almost midnight. I was going to be pushed to get home before my absolute latest getting-back time – twelve-thirty.

"Yeah." Ryan looked uncharacteristically embarrassed. "You know. It's the same person as before."

"Right. Your mystery babe," I said. Lately I'd been wondering if maybe Ryan hadn't just made the girl up. I mean, if she was so fabulous, why didn't he ever bring her out? But I'd seen him pass up chances with other girls so often, just to go off and be with her, that I couldn't quite believe she wasn't real. It suddenly struck me that maybe she was involved with someone else, like Eve had been.

"What's she like?" I said.

Ryan grinned. "Amazing," he said. "Hotter than your wildest dreams. Moody, though. She's in this difficult . . . er . . . situation."

I shook my head. *Jesus*. She *was* going out with someone else.

"Anyway, you coming?" Ryan said.

175

I glanced across the room to where Ella was waiting for me, an inviting smile on her lips.

Screw Eve, I thought. And screw getting home on time. Chloe never does it. Why should I bother?

"Nah, mate," I said. I nodded in Ella's direction. "I'm staying a bit longer."

19

Discovery

No one tells you nothing
Even when you know they know
But they tell you what you should do
They don't like to see you grow

Why don't you ask them – what they expect from you?
Why don't you tell them – what you are gonna do?

'Do Anything You Wanna Do'
Eddie and the Hot Rods

In the end I didn't get home until after two a.m. It wasn't
entirely my fault. Ella had to be back by midnight and her
dad had given her the money for a taxi. I told her to save
it – that I'd walk her home. Of course she lived two miles
away in the middle of nowhere. So once I'd dropped her,
her telephone number in my cell, I had to walk most of the
two miles back before I got near a night-bus that would
take me home.

By this time, I was so close to Kirsty's cousin's house again that I thought I might as well look back in on the party. It was still going – but quieter and emptier. I sat and chatted to a group of Kirsty's cousin's friends who were all staying overnight in the house. One girl, called Sinitta, kept catching my eye.

I thought about Eve. Then I thought about Ella.

Then I thought, why not?

Sinitta was prettier than Ella, but also more irritating. She kept giggling and shying away every time I tried to put my arm around her. I couldn't work out what she wanted. In the end I decided just to be direct.

"So are we gonna pull or not?" I said.

I was half expecting her to slap me or stalk off, all horrified. But to my surprise she just grinned and led me off to a secluded corner of the big, open-plan living room. She was pretty cool, actually. I'm not sure how far we might have gone, but after an hour or so she fell asleep while I went for a pee.

I already had her phone number logged next to Ella's. So I decided to leave. There were a couple of missed calls from Mum, but I figured there was no point me calling her back now. Hopefully by the time I got home she'd have gone to bed. I didn't even think I was going to be that late, but then I waited almost an hour for a night-bus. I guess it sounds really pathetic, but I got all jittery while I was waiting. It'd happened several times since Ben beat me up. I was OK the rest of the time – it was just being outside, at night, when I couldn't see into all the shadows.

The living-room light was on at home as I walked down the road. With any luck that would be Chloe, just come in late herself.

Of course, it wasn't.

Mum flew at me as I opened the front door.

"Luke, I've been so worried. Where've you been? Why are you so late?"

She pulled me into this half-relieved, half-exasperated hug. I struggled free. "I'm fine, Mum," I said, "I've just been to a party."

This was clearly the wrong thing to say. Mum's mouth set in a thin line. The relief in her eyes turned into anger. "You're nearly three hours late back," she hissed. "What were you doing at a party all this time?"

Guessing she wouldn't like the honest answer, I shrugged. "Nothing much."

Again, the wrong thing to say. I could see Matt hovering in the living-room door. He looked massively annoyed.

Mum was holding up her hand, pointing to her forefinger.

"One. You are supposed to be home at half-twelve." She

179

pointed to the next finger. "Two. You have a phone. Why didn't you call? More than that, why didn't you answer when I called?"

I shrugged again, feeling a little uneasy. Truth was I'd turned my phone off when I went back to the party and thought I was in with a chance with Sinitta.

"Three. You were beaten up less than a month ago. D'you have any idea how worried I get when you're out late?"

Shit. Maybe I had been a bit selfish not letting Mum know where I was. Except, I hadn't *meant* not to call her. I just hadn't thought about it. I opened my mouth to explain – to say sorry – but, at that moment, Matt muttered something. I couldn't quite work out what he'd said, but the contempt in his voice was unmistakable.

"What was that?"

Matt sneered. "Selfish little sod."

Something snapped inside me. This was nothing to do with him.

"Why am I getting this crap?" I shouted. "Chloe comes in late all the time. I bet she's not even here now."

"We're not talking about Chloe. We're talking about you," Matt yelled.

I swore at him. This turned out to be my third and final mistake of the evening. Matt sprang forwards and grabbed

180

my shirt, yanking it up by my neck. *Wham*. He shoved me against the door. "Don't you dare use that language with me," he roared.

"Get off." I glared at him, pushing him away with the flats of my hands.

"Matt," Mum shrieked. "Luke. Stop it."

Matt let go of me reluctantly. He raised a shaking finger. "Your dad would be so disappointed in you," he shouted. "You know what he expected? That once he was gone you'd step up – act like a man. Look after your mum. Not drive her half mad with worry."

"Oh yeah?" I yelled. "That what he expected, was it? Well, I can tell you what he *didn't* expect. He didn't expect that his best friend would steal his wife before he'd even been dead three months."

"Luke." Over Matt's shoulder I could see Mum starting to cry.

Matt's face clenched up with fury. "You selfish little bastard. You've got no idea, have you? To you it's all a game. I love your mum. D'you understand? I really love her."

I stared at him, my stomach twisting. It suddenly struck me that Mum might decide she loved him too. That everything might change for ever.

"No, I can see from your face that you don't understand," Matt put his arm round Mum's shoulders. "Your idea of love is to bugger off chasing skirt all night without letting anyone know where you are."

I tore past him and stomped up the stairs. As I slammed my bedroom door shut I could hear Mum and Matt arguing downstairs. I lay on my bed, my heart hammering.

At that moment I would have given everything for five minutes with Eve. And, for once, it wasn't about how horny she was. I just missed her so much it hurt.

I fell asleep and dreamed that she was next to me, holding me while I slept.

I think Matt must have stormed off in the middle of the night, because he wasn't around at all the next morning. Mum's eyes were all red and puffy. I couldn't pretend I wasn't pleased Matt was gone. But I hate it when Mum and I are mad at each other. And despite what Matt said, I *do* try and look after her, now Dad's not here.

So I said I was sorry for staying out late and not calling. We hugged and made up and I offered to peel some potatoes for lunch.

Chloe rolled in just as Mum was about to take a tray of sausages out of the oven.

"Ooh, good, I'm starving," Chloe said, flumping down into one of the kitchen chairs.

I don't know why she acts like that. It's almost as if she

wants to wind Mum up. Of course, Mum immediately launched into her usual stuff about Chloe treating the house like a hotel. Chloe shouted back. And the sausages got burned.

They sniped at each other for most of the afternoon, then Chloe went out again. I had long since given up asking her who she was seeing, or even if it was still the same guy. For all I knew she could have a whole string of boyfriends.

At about six o'clock Mum told me Matt was coming round. From the way she said it, it sounded like they might be going to have a fairly heavy talk. I decided to make myself scarce.

It was a beautiful evening. Still light, with long rays of sunlight stretching across the road. I wandered down to the park where Eve and I used to meet. The trees rustled as I strolled across to the small pond. The park was nearly deserted – nothing and no one to take my mind off Eve. I thought about the last time I'd seen her, hurrying through the corridors at school. I'd wanted to go up to her, talk to her, just be with her.

How could she have chosen Ben? What did he have that I didn't? Well, I knew the answer to that – Ryan had supplied it the first time we'd talked about it.

Ryan. Maybe I should drop in on him. He only lived a

few streets away. And he was always good at looking on the positive side of things. He'd probably tell me to stop being such a sad loser and call Ella or Sinitta.

I glanced down the side path I was passing. Halfway down was a little park bench Eve and I used to sit and make out on. A couple were on there now, arms wrapped round each other. I couldn't see the girl properly. The guy was all over her. From the back there was something familiar about him. Then he turned slightly sideways and I saw who it was. Ryan.

A grin crept round my mouth. Whoever he was with must be his mystery woman. His hotter than hot – possibly otherwise attached – babe of babes. I strode down the path towards them. I walked quietly, wanting to surprise him. Not that I needed to bother. The two of them looked so into each other that they wouldn't have noticed if I'd yelled at them through a megaphone.

I still couldn't see the girl's face. *God, Ryan. Come up for air, why don't you.*

I was still twenty or thirty metres away when he finally pulled away. He leaned back in his seat and I saw who the girl was.

My heart plummeted into my guts. I stopped and stared, unable to believe what I was seeing. Then Ryan gave his lopsided grin and leaned into her again. She hadn't noticed me. She hadn't taken her eyes off Ryan for one second.

As they started snogging again, I sped up.

His hands were all over her.

I raced down the path towards them, my head exploding with rage.

20
Twisted

Walked out this morning
Don't believe what I saw
A hundred billion bottles
Washed up on the shore
Seems I'm not alone in being alone
A hundred billion castaways looking for a home

'Message in a Bottle'
The Police

They didn't notice me running. I was right on top of them and they still didn't see.

I lunged forwards, grabbed Ryan's jacket at the back and hauled him off her.

"You bastard," I yelled, hurling him onto the gravel path below the park bench.

I turned and stared at the girl.

Chloe.

Her mouth was open, her eyes wide.

Ryan picked himself off the gravel and turned round to face me.

"Hey, Luke, you've got this all wrong."

"Don't . . . don't you dare speak to me." My voice was shaking. My whole body was trembling with anger. "I told you not to mess about with my sister."

Ryan held his arms out, palms down, gesturing me to chill.

"I'm not messing about, man. Chloe's *her*. The girl I told you about. We've been going out for a bit now and—"

"Chloe?" I frowned, my brain straining to catch up with my ears. "My sister's your . . . your mystery babe?"

"Yeah." Ryan nodded, beckoning Chloe towards him.

I stared at him, still struggling to make sense of what he was saying. "When?" I said. "When did it start?"

"Pig off, Luke," Chloe snapped. "We don't owe you an explan—"

"It's OK, Chlo." Ryan turned to me. "It started just after your party," he said. "When I came round that night to help you . . . you know."

The evening he'd told me about the Six Steps. My eyes widened.

"*That's* why you came up to me back at the party? *That's* why you acted all friendly? Just to get your hands on Chloe?"

"No." Ryan backed away from me. "Honest, Luke."

He was lying. *Bastard. Bastard. Bastard.*

I shoved him in the chest, knocking him back onto the ground. He landed with a thud. I threw myself on top of him and swung my fist back. I was dimly aware of Chloe tugging at my arm, screeching in my ear, but the words were lost under the furious sound of the blood pumping through my head. It was like all my rage, all my frustration – at Matt and Mum, at Eve, at Ben – was focused in this one moment.

Ryan was trying to scrabble backwards along the ground, but my knees were pinning down his arms. My fist itched to drive itself into his stupid face.

Then the rest of the world rushed back into focus. I suddenly became aware of my own harsh breathing – and the swishing sound of the trees in the background.

I opened my trembling fingers and lowered my arm. The truth flooded through me. If I hit Ryan, I'd be as bad as Ben.

And I was better than that.

Way better.

"Listen." Ryan's eyes pleaded with me.

I sat back, then rolled onto the gravel path beside him. I was still panting, my heart still racing. I bent over my knees.

"Go on then," I said. "This should be good."

Ryan struggled onto his elbows. "I didn't know what

else to do," he said. "I'd liked Chloe for ages. But she was always surrounded by guys. I could never get near her. Not at school. Not even at the party."

"But I saw you dancing with someone else that night," I said. "And there was that girl – the one with red hair. I saw you kiss her . . ."

"What else was I gonna do?" Ryan shrugged. "But you gotta believe me. I'd've swapped it all for two minutes on my own with Chloe."

"So you *did* use me?" I said. "That's why you came round. Why you kept coming round." I blinked, remembering the way Ryan had demonstrated his stupid "look" on Chloe. And the way he was always supposedly nipping up to our bathroom every time he visited. Our bathroom, which just happened to be next door to Chloe's bedroom.

"At first, yes, OK. But then, later, I liked hanging out with you." Ryan looked at me earnestly. "I would have told you, man. Chloe wanted to. She didn't think it was a big deal. But the way you acted when I looked at her that time – remember? It totally freaked me out. I thought if you knew what I was doing you'd be mad." He gave me a weak smile. "Which you obviously are. But I wasn't trying to upset you. I just wanted to be with Chlo."

My head reeled.

"Are you OK?" Chloe stroked Ryan's cheek. There was

real concern in her eyes. I'd never seen her look like that at anyone.

He nodded, turning his mouth so he could kiss her fingers.

My temper rose. "Whoa," I said fiercely. "Enough." I turned to Chloe. I had to make her see Ryan was a total chancer. That he'd hit on anything that moved.

"He goes after girls all the time, Chlo. Once I was at his house and he had someone up in his room that his mum didn't even know about."

"That was me, you idiot. I spend loads of time at Ryan's house. And I've met his mum. We get on really well."

I frowned. "But . . . but . . . he tells lies." I remembered what Ryan had said to her that first evening. "Like about his stepdad being dead."

"I know," Chloe said. "I know. He apologised for lying about it the second time we talked. He did it to make me notice him. I know what he's like, Luke."

"No," I said. "You don't know what he's like. I mean, he's always horning after girls. Always. I've been to parties with him where he's chatted up every girl in the room."

"But I never *do* anything," Ryan protested. He turned towards Chloe and stroked her hair. "Of course I talk to girls. I love girls. They're much more interesting than boys. But it's just flirting." He moved closer to Chloe. "I can't wait to get back and see you."

190

Chloe was gazing at him with big, stupid eyes. I couldn't believe it. She had totally fallen for Ryan's act. And he was laughing at her, just like he'd been laughing at me all along.

"No." I leaned over him again and pushed him away from her. He scrambled back, getting to his feet, his hands in the air in front of him.

I stood up, racking my brains for an example of Ryan going after some other girl. "What about that one at that party a few weeks ago?" I said. "She had long, dark hair, Chlo. And they were massively flirting and then he followed her out of the room."

Ryan laughed. "Only so I could walk straight out of the house. I knew you'd think I was going off with her. All I could think about that night was getting back to Chloe."

Jesus. My temper was rising again. Ryan had an answer for everything. What really bugged me was that – when I thought about it – it was true. I'd never actually seen him getting off with anyone since our party. But, then, he wouldn't have let me see, just in case I found out about Chloe. I gritted my teeth. Nothing was going to convince me that he hadn't snogged that dark-haired girl – even if he'd left afterwards.

"Luke," Chloe pleaded. "Ryan's your friend. He worked his arse off convincing people you hadn't touched Eve."

"Only so's he could touch you," I snapped, suddenly

realising at last why Ryan had stood up for me. "He didn't do that for me. He did it to impress you."

I shoved Ryan in the chest. He stumbled backwards a couple of steps. I was itching for him to swing a punch at me, so I could hit him back.

"Luke," Chloe shouted.

But Ryan just grinned. "I'm not going to hit you, Luke. You're her brother." He glanced at Chloe, then back at me. "But I'm not stopping going out with Chloe either."

My chest tightened. In that moment I hated Ryan.

I hated the way Chloe was looking at him, like a knight in shining armour. I hated the way he was smiling at me. And most of all, I hated the way he was so obviously convinced that, as usual, he could talk his way out of anything.

Which was when I realised exactly how to make Chloe see just how cynical he was.

I turned to her. "He's got this stupid method, Chloe, that he boasts about. Six Steps that'll get you any girl. And he's got a load of photos of him with all the girls he's been out with because of them. They're just numbers to him."

I glared at her triumphantly, confident she would look appalled and turn accusingly on Ryan. But Chloe just shook her head sadly at me.

I felt Ryan's hand on my shoulder. "Those girls are just

mates. And the Six Steps are bollocks, man. I told Chloe about them already. For a laugh."

I stared at him, bewildered.

"It was Tones," Ryan said. "He used to mope around all the time going on about Kirsty. I felt sorry for him, wanted to help – but you know, he's not the sharpest knife in the drawer, so I thought if I gave him like a step-by-step guide to work on, it might make it easier."

I frowned. But the Six Steps had worked. What was he talking about?

"Tones told Numbers about it and Numbers started pestering me for what I'd said, so I told him too. Not that he ever bothered to act on very much of it. And he wildly exaggerates the numbers of girls he gets off with. But that's all it was. Just a few ideas to help Tones get Kirsty to go out with him."

I swallowed. The sun had completely gone in now and a chill breeze rippled across the small pond.

Ryan smiled. "There is no masterplan for getting a girl. I wish there was. I mean there are things you can do or not do that may make a difference. But sometimes you can try and try and they never notice you exist and sometimes you meet someone and you both just know you're meant to be together."

He took Chloe's hand.

I watched them lean against each other. And I realised it wasn't really Ryan I was angry with. It was Eve.

Eve.

Why was everything, always, all about Eve?

There was a long pause.

"Having said all that . . ." Ryan grinned. ". . . I am considering setting up a dating consultancy when I leave school." He started to back away, pulling Chloe with him along the gravel path. His grin broadened. "I think I'd make a million, helping sad cases like you."

I stared at him, my anger flaring again. And then, suddenly, it hit me how funny it was. All my efforts to get Eve to notice me. And all the time Ryan was doing the same thing, getting Chloe to notice him.

"Watch who you're calling sad, numbnuts," I growled. "You're stuck with *her*."

"Hey." Chloe's voice rose, querulously.

I could see the relief on Ryan's face. He was still backing away up the gravel path, holding Chloe's hand. Our eyes met.

Oh well, I thought. She could have a worse boyfriend.

I grinned, and followed them up the path.

21

Home

And you're standing here beside me
And I love the passing of time
Never for money
Always for love

'This Must be the Place'
Talking Heads

Home was transformed now that Mum and everyone at school knew Chloe was going out with Ryan. Don't get me wrong, Chloe was still moody and rude. And she still went out all the time, which Mum got well strung-out over, as she was supposed to be revising for her GCSEs.

But she was calmer too. And there were fewer rows.

Ryan came round most nights now after school – either to see her or to pick her up to go out. That first day after I'd found them together he just marched in, went up to Mum and announced he was Chloe's boyfriend. I think Mum was a bit stunned – though flattered when he started in on how nice her hair looked and how pretty her cardigan was.

The next day he turned up on the doorstep when Mum was making beans on toast. Matt was taking her to some show with a really late dinner afterwards and she wanted a snack before they went out.

She'd made loads as both Chloe and I said we were starving.

I let Ryan in and walked back into the kitchen with him. As soon as Chloe saw him, she stood up.

"I'm off out," she said.

Mum, who was dishing up the food on the counter, turned round. "Chloe," she sighed. "What about your food?"

"Changed my mind."

I could see Mum was upset. I glanced at Ryan.

He was frowning at Chloe. "We've got time to eat, Chlo," he said.

"Not hungry," she said, swooping towards the door.

Ryan stuck out his arm to stop her leaving. He stared at her. "If you asked for the food you should eat it."

There was a deathly silence. Mum and I looked at each other. I knew we were both waiting for the explosion from Chloe. If either of us had said that to her, she would have gone mental.

But instead she turned and went back to the table. "OK," she said. "Thanks, Mum. Maybe I will have some."

Mum nearly dropped the saucepan.

When Chloe had finished, Ryan took the plate up to the counter.

On his way out of the kitchen, he bent over and whispered something in Mum's ear. After the front door had shut behind them, I turned to her.

"What did he say?"

Mum grinned at me. "He said: 'I know she's a handful. I'm working on it.'"

I nearly went to the after-school Art Club on Thursday. Even got as far as the door. But then I pictured Eve's face on the other side of it. Eve, sitting there, laughing and beautiful. Working on her project. Sending me sexy glances. Waiting for the end of the class so we could put on the radio and dance . . . and kiss . . . and . . .

But none of that was going to happen. So I left and walked home.

Why did I still miss her so badly?

I called Ella and Sinitta. I went out with both of them on different days. Just to the pictures. I liked them. I did.

But when I closed my eyes and kissed them, I wanted it to be Eve.

It was another two weeks before I saw her properly. She was right across the playground from me, chatting to her friends. I stared at her. I know it wasn't cool. But I couldn't help myself.

She was just so beautiful. So effortlessly, sexily beautiful.

She must have felt me staring because she looked up. She smiled at me, but I couldn't smile back. Then she started walking towards me. I kept looking at her all the time, watching her glide closer and closer. Then she stopped.

"You don't come to the after-school Art Club anymore," she said. "I thought maybe you'd come back, finish your project?"

I said nothing.

I'd like to tell you I was being aloof. In fact, I didn't have a clue what to say. Why was she banging on about that stupid button thing again?

"Maybe I'll see you there?" Eve said.

And then I got it. She was happy with how things had turned out. She wanted to be friends.

"I doubt it," I said. And I strode off, leaving her standing there.

The next day was Saturday, the beginning of April. The school term ended next week and Mum had chosen today to scatter Dad's ashes. She'd decided to take them up to this old woodland near where Dad grew up. Unlike the funeral, she wanted to keep it as just us. Of course Matt was included, as he was Dad's best friend, so, naturally, Chloe wanted to bring Ryan. Mum put up a token fuss for about five minutes but, to be honest, I think she likes it better when Ry's around. He's certainly the only person I know who can even begin to handle Chloe.

Nobody thought to ask me whether I was going to feel like a spare part being the only one without a partner. Still, I didn't care all that much. It was just a trip in the car to some woods. A chance to think about Eve. I couldn't see why everyone thought it was so important. I mean, Dad died months ago. I hadn't thought about him an awful lot since then, and I hadn't felt much at his funeral. I couldn't see that today would be very different.

When we got there, Mum took the wooden box full of Dad's ashes and we walked through some trees. It was a dull day, quite cloudy, but warm. The trees were all covered in green leaves and bursting buds and the trunks were sticky with sap.

We came to this little clearing surrounded by beautiful trees with white and silver trunks. Mum stopped and we huddled in a little circle. "I don't know what to say . . ." Mum hesitated. "But today feels like we're really saying goodbye." She squeezed my hand and tipped some of the ashes out of the box. Then she handed it to Matt. He did the same thing and passed the box to Chloe.

Clinging to Ryan and weeping, Chloe took the box and shook it gently. Ashes floated to the ground.

"Bye Dad," she whispered. "I love you."

And then she passed the box to me. I took it, my heart suddenly beating fast. There were only a few ashes still inside the box. Was that all that was left? Of a man? Of his life?

No. He was coming back. He'd always been coming back before.

I stood rigid. Completely still. But inside I was wild with panic. There had to be a mistake. I wasn't ready to say goodbye. I tried to remember Dad's face but it kept slipping away, like I was seeing it through a fog. I closed my eyes, concentrating harder, willing him into my head.

And then I saw him. How he used to look when we played football and he scored a goal – running around, grinning, with his arms in the air. How he sat in his chair when he was ill, his eyes empty and sad, staring at the TV.

How he'd listened to music. All the time. *God*. How he'd tried to get me to listen with him before he died.

I opened my eyes and stared at the handful of ashes in the box, not wanting to let them go. I tipped the box. Not much. Just a little. But enough for the wind to whip inside and whirl the ashes up and out into the air.

They floated to the ground.

This wave of loss welled up through my gut. I bent over, trying to hold it in. But it pushed up and up, through my chest and into my throat. I had to let it out. It was too big, too powerful to hold inside me any longer.

It ripped itself out of me in this awful, tearing wail. My legs buckled. I dropped the empty box and fell forwards onto my knees. My hands clawed at ash and earth. Dust trickled through my fingers.

I curled over on the ground and howled. Tears and snot and spit and rage spilled out of me.

I pressed my face into the earth, surrendering to the pain of it.

My dad was dead.

He was never coming back.

I don't know how long I lay there. But when I finally looked up, the clearing was empty. No. Not quite empty. Mum was sitting on the ground a couple of metres away, her legs curled up underneath her, her back against one of the silver trees.

She smiled, her eyes full of tears. "Luke?"

I brushed the dirt from my face and sat up, my face

burning. How could I have completely lost it like that? In front of everyone. I stared at the earth.

"Are you all right?" Mum's voice was sad, hesitant. "Do you want to talk?"

I shook my head. We sat in silence for a moment. A soft breeze rustled through the trees, cool against my face. I felt lighter, somehow. And yet . . . less empty.

"Where did everyone go?"

"Back to the car," Mum said. "I thought you'd rather be on your own, but . . . but I . . ." Her voice cracked.

I looked up. A tear was trickling down her face. Her mouth trembled. "Oh, Luke."

I got up and walked over to her. I sat down beside her and hugged her. And maybe . . . you know, maybe I did cry a little more. I mean, I'm sorry if you think that's lame, but he was my dad.

After a while Mum pulled back and blew her nose. "I'm sorry I didn't realise how hard all this was for you. I've been so worried about Chloe that I didn't . . . I mean, I know she's better now . . . now that Ryan's around, but still . . ."

Ryan.

My face flushed. How embarrassing, wailing like that in front of Ryan.

Mum seemed to read my mind. "Ryan'll understand."

She blew her nose again. "He's your friend. It's you I'm worried about."

"I'm fine, Mum." I stood up and held out my hand to help her up. Maybe she was right. Ryan was pretty cool about emotional stuff.

Mum reached out her own hand to take mine and I suddenly remembered doing the same thing with Dad, just before he went into hospital the last time. He'd been sitting in his armchair and was trying to get up. And he was too weak, so I'd gone over and held out my hand to help him. And he'd let me pull him up and then he'd hugged me. He didn't say anything, just held me really tightly. And I'd been all embarrassed, because Dad and I didn't do that kind of stuff. Hugging and that.

Funny how I'd forgotten it and now it was such a strong memory I could almost feel his body, all weak and wasted, under my arms.

Dad hadn't wanted to go away. He hadn't wanted to leave me. He just hadn't known what to say.

And I hadn't known what to say to him.

And now it was too late.

"Luke?" Mum brushed the hair off my forehead.

"Really, I'm fine, Mum." I leaned forward and kissed her on the cheek. "Er . . . thanks."

She frowned. "Thanks for what?"

I shrugged. "Dunno," I said. "Just 'thanks'."

Mum's frown smoothed out into a smile.

"Come on," she said. "Let's go back to the car."

And together we strolled through the trees, the wind pushing at the branches, waving us towards the path.

22

Free

What set you free
And brought you to me, babe
What set you free
I need you here by me

'Rebel Yell'
Billy Idol

We got home at about four. The sun had finally managed to burn through the clouds and the house felt stuffy.

I went upstairs and played all Dad's records, one by one. For the first time, I listened properly. To the music. To the words. Some of them I liked. Some of them I didn't. But that didn't matter. They were his. And he'd wanted to share them with me.

I was still upstairs when the doorbell rang. My door was open and I could hear Mum talking to whoever it was, asking them if they wanted to come in.

Then the door shut and Mum yelled up to me. "Luke, something here for you."

I sauntered downstairs. Mum was holding out a small envelope. My name was printed on it in bold, black capitals. "Chloe's friend, Eve, was just here," she said. "But not to see Chloe. She didn't want to come in. Just said she was dropping off something of yours, something to do with an art project?"

The world stood still. I took the envelope and ripped it open. Inside were a handful of wooden buttons. They clanked, dully, against each other. There was no note. Nothing.

"Did she say anything else?" I stared at Mum, my heart pounding.

Mum shook her head. "What does—?"

But I was already out the door.

On the pavement, I looked up and down the road. Where was she? Then I saw her. Almost at the corner. I raced after her.

"Eve," I yelled. "Eve."

She stopped. Turned round. I panted up to her, my eyes drinking in her face. She looked nervous.

"What . . .?" I faltered. "Why . . .?"

"I thought you might want your buttons back, as you're not coming to Art Club anymore," she said.

I frowned.

"My coursework's coming on well," she said, "I've done a collage of both my mum's eyes now. Took me ages to get them so they looked abstract, not crossed."

"Eve?" *What's going on? Why are you here?*

There was a long silence. A single ray of sunlight fell between us across the pavement.

Eve's mouth trembled. "I dumped Ben," she said. "A week ago. You were right, all he cared about was what his mates thought. He told me he'd only been going out with me because everyone thought I was hot. And that he was going to dump me anyway because I wouldn't . . . you know . . . do it with him." She glanced away. "He asked me not to say anything for a few days, so I didn't. Then, yesterday, he started telling people he'd dumped *me*."

I took a step closer to her. "He's a piece of work," I said. "You should forget him."

She looked up at me. "I have," she said.

There was another long silence.

I couldn't bear it. What was she telling me? What was she asking me?

"So . . .?" I said.

Eve stepped into the ray of sunlight between us. She put up her hand to shield her eyes from the glare. "You were right to make me choose," she stammered. "I mean I was

207

angry at the time. I told myself you were arrogant and stupid . . . but it made me realise . . . stuff." She took a deep breath. "A lot of what it came down to was that I was embarrassed what people would think . . . what they'd say . . . you know . . . if I dated someone so much younger."

"I'm not so much younger. My birthday's in September. That's just six months diff—"

"It's a different school year. Oh, Luke, you know what people are like. I thought they'd talk about me behind my back. Or tease me about it."

"So all you care about is what other people think?" I said, slowly.

Jesus. Was that it?

"Chloe's going out with Ryan. He's in my year and she doesn't seem bothered."

Eve took her hand away from her face. Her eyes were paler than ever in the glare of the sun. "I know. It was really stupid of me. You're a million times cuter than Ben. And you make me laugh. And you really listen to what I say . . ." She bit her lip. "Anyway, I guess now you know what a jerk I am you won't want to come back to Art Club."

Bloody hell. Why was she dragging up Art Club again? Why couldn't she say what she meant?

"You mean, you want to be friends?" I said, uncertainly.

"If that's what you want." She shrugged.

I stared at her, my throat suddenly tight. "What do *you* want?" I said.

She stepped out of the sunlight towards me. "I miss you," she said. "And I don't care what people think anymore."

She just stood there staring up at me.

She was like nobody else.

And she wanted me.

I hesitated for less than a second.

Her cheek felt warm under my cold fingers. Her lips soft on my mouth. I leaned into her, feeling myself falling.

Letting myself fall.

We started going out properly after that. Mostly on our own or in big groups, but sometimes double-dating with Chlo and Ryan. Chloe was a bit sniffy at first, but once Eve told everyone in her year Ben had forced her into saying I'd attacked her, Chloe forgave her everything. And, as expected, Ben was too busy with his new girlfriend to be the slightest bit bothered about Eve and me.

We get on well, the four of us. Ry and Chloe both love being the centre of attention, while me and Eve are happy to sit back and let them get on with it. Frankly, watching

Ryan talk Chloe out of a mood is a whole evening's worth of entertainment in its own right.

But after a while, I always draw Eve away, get her to myself for a bit. She's been teased at school for dating me, but she's still here.

What else can I tell you?

Maybe just this: A few days ago Chloe gave me part of the letter Dad left for her when he died. It's about me.

. . . it comes down to this – it's easier to write to you, Chloe, because you're not so much like me . . . but with Luke it's like looking in a mirror. I want to write to him, to tell him how proud I am of him and how much I love him – but he already knows those things. And the truth is, I don't trust myself not to make the letter about me – mistakes and regrets and ambitions etc. And I don't want to give him anything to live up to – or down to, for that matter. That's why I've left him the records. I hope they'll help him understand that I've been through so many of the same things he is, has and will go through too. And that I love him so much and trust him to find his own life. To make his own way.

I showed Eve. Only Eve. She read it and hugged me.

You see, she totally gets me.

Totally gets who I am and what I want.

My girl.

My life.

My way.

Turn over for a taste
of the next book
in the series,
Three's a Crowd!

1
The plan

D'you want to know the worst thing about having a totally amazing girlfriend?

What's he on about, you're asking? How can there be a worst thing? How can there even be a downside? Especially with Eve. She's beautiful and sexy and fun and sweet.

And she likes me back.

Well, there *is* a downside.

It's all the other guys. The ones who wish they were with her instead of me.

I guess she gets about six boys a day hitting on her. And that's just an ordinary school day. If we go to a party or a club I can't leave her for a minute without them swarming round her like wasps.

Drives me mad.

Eve doesn't see it. She says they're just chatting. Being friendly. But I know better. I know they don't care about her, like I do. I know they're just after one thing.

Most blokes are like that. Eve's previous boyfriend, Ben, was always trying to get her to do it with him. Yeah, Ben. He didn't like it when he found out I'd been seeing Eve.

But that's another story. I don't want to think about all that. I just want to think about Eve.

Eve and me.

It was the last week of the summer term. Eve and I were meeting after school in the Burger Bar. I like it there – they play good music and sell big portions at cheap prices.

I walked in a bit late, thanks to a heated discussion with my form teacher who says if I don't work harder I'm going to fail all my GCSEs next year. I saw Eve straight away. I always see her first in any room. That's not some weird, psychic connection by the way. It's her hair. Catches the light – all sleek and blonde.

She was sitting at one of the booths, her head bent over a plastic sheet menu. I could just make out someone else's arm on the other side of the table. A male arm. Whoever it was must have been sitting slouched down – I couldn't see his head and shoulders – but there was definitely someone there. Someone flirting with her. As usual.

I strode over, psyching myself up for the necessary *get-out-of-here-this-is-my-girlfriend* look I was about to give.

Then I saw who it was. Ryan. I breathed a sigh of relief.

Ryan's pretty much my best mate. He's going out with my older sister, Chloe. In fact that's how we got to know each other – when he was after Chlo and I was after Eve a few months ago.

"Hi, Luke." Ryan grinned up at me from his bench. "Eve and I were just talking about you."

"Oh, yeah?" I looked over at Eve. She was blushing, like Ryan had really embarrassed her. She had to have the sexiest, poutiest mouth in the history of the world.

I couldn't look at that mouth without wanting to kiss it.

I slid in beside her and leaned across. *Mmmn.*

I could hear Ryan making puking noises across the table. I didn't care. Eve pushed me gently away. Her eyes sparkled up at me.

"So what were you saying about me?" I asked.

"Um . . ." Eve looked away.

"Wait till Chloe gets here." Ryan nudged Eve across the table. "I've just called her. She'll be here any minute."

I frowned, wondering what was going on. Then Eve took my hand and I forgot everything else.

"You're here early," I said. This was a running joke between us. Eve is always, always late for everything.

"I *was* early, actually." Eve smiled.

"Eve has news," Ryan said, looking like he was trying not to laugh.

"What?" I said.

"Wait for Chloe," Ryan said again.

"Jesus, Ry. What's going on?"

"Come on, man. You know Chloe. She'll be furious if she's left out of it."

This was undoubtedly true, though not what I was asking. Chloe's not a bad sister. But she's an unbelievably moody human being. Ryan is the only person I know who has any kind of influence over her. And even he struggles sometimes.

It was at this point that Chloe turned up.

Ryan smiled. "Hey Pig Baby," he drawled in an exaggerated American accent.

"Hi, Skankface." Chloe grinned as she leaned over to kiss him.

Eve and I exchanged glances. Neither of us really get the way Ry and Chloe seem to enjoy being rude to each other. Sometimes they even have these terrible rows, where one or both of them completely lose it. You think they'll never speak again. But the next time you see them, they're back to being all loved-up.

Eve and I don't do that. We're totally into each other. Always.

"So what's this big deal news?" I said.

"It's my dad," Eve said. "He wants me to spend the whole of August at his new hotel in Mallorca."

I blinked at her, my stomach twisting into a knot. "The *whole* of August?"

"Yeah." Eve stared down at the table. I guessed she knew what I was thinking. A whole month apart. And I was so looking forwards to having loads of time together – the summer holidays about to start. And now we'd have . . . what . . . ten days before the end of July – then she'd have to go.

"Sounds cool," Chloe said. "Will your dad expect you to work at the hotel?"

Ryan broke into a fit of coughing.

"Yeah," Eve explained, still staring at the table. "I'll have to help out waiting tables and sorting things out by the pool and maybe even working in the crèche . . . but I guess it's still four weeks in Spain."

My heart was sliding down into my shoes. I was wrong. Four weeks away from me and she didn't even seem all that bothered.

Ryan recovered from his coughing fit.

"Does your dad run the place, then?" he said.

Eve nodded.

"Lots of staff?"

"Yeah – especially over the summer. He gets masses of English tourists, so. . ."

". . .he has to hire extra help," Chloe finished. She raised her eyebrows. "Mmmn. Imagine the buff Spanish pool boys."

I glared at her.

"Bet the girls are hot, too," Ryan added. "Go on, Eve."

Eve paused. "Actually my dad doesn't usually hire girls to work for him. He says they're too distracting for the male staff. And sometimes there are problems with the guests too. You know, middle-aged men trying it on. It's supposed to be a family place, so my dad tries to . . . to stop trouble starting by not hiring girls."

"Yet he's happy for *you* to go and work there?" I said, unable to control the angry shake in my voice. The idea of Eve being away for four weeks was bad enough. But knowing she'd be the only girl working in a hotel full of hot, pervy, Spanish guys and lecherous British tourists was unbearable."What about your mum? Won't she mind?"

But I already knew the answer to that. Eve's mum was nice, but basically pathetic. As far as I could gather from the stories Eve told me, she'd never stood up to Eve's dad once.

Eve wouldn't meet my eyes. I stared at her, Ryan and Chloe forgotten. Her lips twitched. Was she laughing at me?

I sprang to my feet, feeling utterly humiliated. "Great," I said sarcastically. "Hope you have a great time. Send me a postcard."

I turned to walk away. Eve grabbed my wrist.

"Luke," she said. "Stop. We're just messing around."

I turned back to her, pulling my arm free. "What?"

I caught sight of Ryan and Chloe – they were leaning against each other, shaking with silent laughter.

"I'm sorry," Eve said. "Listen, my dad loves girls." She blushed. "Too much, in fact. I certainly won't be the only one working there. But that's not the point."

"I don't get it." I looked from her to Ryan and Chloe.

"Sorry, man." Ryan grinned. "It was my idea. I called Chloe and told her before you arrived."

"But . . . ?"

"For goodness sake, Luke," Chloe sighed. "You are so easy. I mean, have you ever heard of a hotel that refuses to employ women?"

I shrugged, my face burning. It's not that I can't take a joke. I just don't like people taking the piss out of the way I feel about Eve.

Especially when Eve does it.

"That's not all," Eve reached out for my arm again. "Luke?" I looked at her. Her face was stricken. "I'm really sorry. Listen, it's brilliant. My dad said I could bring some friends if I wanted. That's the real news."

"What is?" I said.

"We're all invited. You, me, Ry and Chloe. Dad said it

was okay. I mean, we'll have to do a bit of work while we're there, but we'll have loads of free time. The staff are mostly around our age and the hotel's got a virtually private beach. He says it's beautiful."

I sat down slowly, letting Eve wrap her arms round my neck.

"You mean we're *all* going, for all four weeks?" Relief was seeping through my feelings of anger and humiliation, washing them away.

Eve nodded, her eyes sleepily, sexily, inviting me to kiss her.

A smile crept round my mouth.

"If Mum says it's okay," Chloe said.

I drank in Eve's face again. "Oh, I'm sure that's not going to be a problem." I moved closer to her lips, suddenly feeling exhilarated. This was better than my wildest dreams. A whole month with Eve. In the same building. Not even having to go home at night. And August in Spain. It would be hot and. . .

"Luke." Chloe's voice barged into my mental picture of Eve sprawled across a beach in a bikini.

"What?" I said irritably.

"Put it away, dumb ass. The waitress is waiting to take your order."

Acknowledgements

Thanks, as ever, to Moira, Gaby, Julie, Melanie and Sharon. Also to Daisy Startup and to my editor, Venetia Gosling.

Chapter 1
'My Way' – The Sex Pistols
Words and music written by
Anka/Revaux/Francois/Thibault. Published by Warner
Chappell Music Publishing © 1977. All rights reserved.

Chapter 2
'Is She Really Going Out With Him?' – Joe Jackson
Words and music written by Jackson. Published by Sony
and ATV © 1978. All rights reserved.

Chapter 3
'Ever Fallen in Love?' – Buzzcocks
Words and music written by Shelley. Published by
Complete Music Publishing © 1978. All rights reserved.

Chapter 4
'Cool for Cats' – Squeeze
Words and music written by Tilbrook/Difford. Published
by Rondor Music Publishing © 1978. All rights reserved.

Chapter 9
'Uncertain Smile' – The The
Words and music written by Johnson. Published by
Complete Music Publishing © 1982.

Chapter 10
'Should I Stay Or Should I Go?' – The Clash
Words and music written by Strummer/Jones. Published by
Universal Music Publishing © 1981.

Chapter 11
'Love Song' – The Damned
Words and music written by Millar/Burns/Vanian/Ward.
Published by Rock Music Company Ltd © 1979.

Chapter 12
'Hand in Glove' – The Smiths
Words and music written by Marr/Morrissey. Published
by Warner Chappell and Universal Music Publishing ©
1983.

Chapter 13
'Happy House' – Siouxsie and the Banshees
Words written by Siouxie Sioux. Published by

Chapter 14
'Watching the Detectives' – Elvis Costello and the
Attractions

Chapter 15
'Down in the Tube Station at Midnight' – The Jam

Chapter 16
'Grey Day' – Madness

Chapter 17
'In-between Days' – The Cure

Chapter 18
'The Love Parade' – The Undertones
Words and music written by
Sharkey/O'Neill/Bradley/Doherty. Published by
Universal Music Publishing © 1983.

Chapter 19
'Do Anything You Wanna Do' – Eddie and the Hot Rods
Words and music written by Hollis/Graeme. Published
by Universal Music Publishing and Rock Music
Company Ltd.

Chapter 20
'Message in a Bottle' – The Police
Words and music written by Sting. Published by
Magnetic Music © 1979.

Chapter 21
'This Must Be The Place' – Talking Heads
Words and music by Byrne/Frantz/Harrison/Weymouth.
Published by Warner Chappell Music Publishing © 1983.

Chapter 22
'Rebel Yell' – Billy Idol
Words written by Idol. Published by Bone Idol
Music/Chrysalis Music Ltd © 1983. Used by permission.
All rights reserved.

Falling

Fast

"romantic
and heart-
wrenching"
CHICKLISH

SOPHIE
McKENZIE

This is life, not a rehearsal

When River auditions for a part in an inter-school
performance of Romeo and Juliet, she finds herself
smitten by Flynn, the boy playing Romeo. River
believes in romantic love, and she can't wait to
experience it. But Flynn comes from a damaged
family - is he even capable of giving River what she
wants? The path of true love never did run smooth...

ISBN 978-0-85707-099-9 £6.99

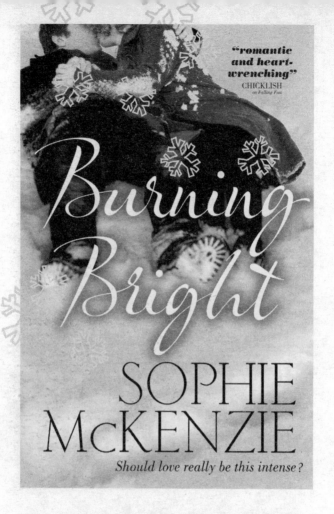

> "romantic
> and heart-
> wrenching"
> CHICKLISH
> on Falling Fast

Burning Bright

SOPHIE McKENZIE

Should love really be this intense?

Four months have passed and River and Flynn's
romance is still going strong. River thinks Flynn has
his anger under control, but when she discovers he
has been getting into fights and is facing a terrible
accusation at school, she starts to question both
Flynn's honesty - and the intensity of their passion.
Things come to a head at a family get together
when River sees Flynn fly into one unprovoked
rage too many. The consequences for both of them
are devastating and threaten to tear them apart
forever.

ISBN 978-0-85707-101-9 £6.99

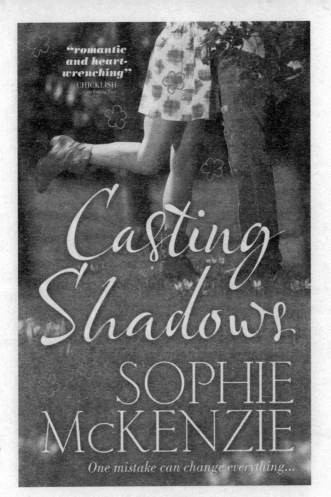

"romantic and heart-wrenching"
CHICKLISH
on *Falling Fast*

Casting Shadows

SOPHIE McKENZIE

One mistake can change everything...

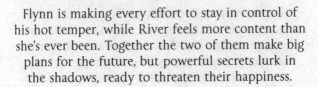

Flynn is making every effort to stay in control of his hot temper, while River feels more content than she's ever been. Together the two of them make big plans for the future, but powerful secrets lurk in the shadows, ready to threaten their happiness.

ISBN 978-0-85707-103-3 £6.99

"romantic and heart-wrenching"
CHICKLISH

Defy
the
Stars

SOPHIE
McKENZIE

Together at last – whatever it costs?

After months apart, everyone thinks that River is successfully building a future without Flynn. Indeed, she has almost convinced herself that she is moving on. And then, one day, Flynn is back, bringing with him tales of his glamorous new life. River suspects his lucrative new work involves some form of criminal activity, but will she let herself be drawn back into Flynn's world? Or is this, finally, the end of the line for them both?

ISBN 978-0-85707-105-7 £6.99